THE

'*I want experienced nurses only.*' Dr Paul Konrad's arrogant statement was not calculated to please the clinical teacher Sister Julia Carr. She had counted on letting her student nurses learn from his research into ways of preventing heart disease and she was quite prepared to do battle, even though his aura of ruthlessness nearly made her resolution falter!

Hazel Fisher is a trained psychiatric nurse but has also worked on medical and surgical wards in general hospitals. She draws on her own nursing experiences to provide the background for her novels, supplemented where necessary by careful research. She is half-Geordie but has spent most of her life in Sussex, and now lives in a pretty little village nestling at the foot of the South Downs. She enjoys reading and writing Doctor Nurse Romances, and believes they educate, as well as entertain the reader, and provide some much-needed escapism.

THE HEART SPECIALIST

BY

HAZEL FISHER

MILLS & BOON LIMITED
15–16 BROOK'S MEWS
LONDON W1A 1DR

*First published in Great Britain 1986
by Mills & Boon Limited*

© Hazel Fisher 1986

*Australian copyright 1986
Philippine copyright 1986*

ISBN 0 263 75483 9

Set in 10 on 12 pt Linotron Times
03–0886–53,000

*Photoset by Rowland Phototypesetting Limited
Bury St Edmunds, Suffolk
Made and printed in Great Britain by
William Collins Sons & Company Limited
Glasgow*

CHAPTER ONE

'Is this the list of new students?' asked Sister Julia Carr, picking up a neatly-typed sheet of quarto.

'Mm, that's right.' Sister Wendy Hamilton smiled at the senior clinical teacher. 'There are fifteen hopefuls for us in the new set. They seemed a bright lot at interview, anyway—keen and raring to go!'

They exchanged amused glances. 'They always *are* keen,' Julia commented, pushing back a strand of red-gold hair that had escaped the confines of her neat chignon. 'All too often the keenness doesn't last the first month.'

'I've no doubt you'll spur them on to greater things!' laughed Wendy.

'Fame is the spur,' Julia murmured. 'Which one do I have to watch out for?' she asked, scanning the list. She turned puzzled deep blue eyes on her friend. 'The Principal Tutor said one of them is almost Royalty! She was joking, I hope?'

Wendy pulled a face. 'Well—yes and no. One of the set, Sally Dalton, is a protégée of the new visiting consultant. He encouraged her to apply to St Crispin's and he'll be keeping an eye on her progress. I think her mother is a close friend, if you know what I mean.'

'I hope he isn't going to interfere. Consultants must be kept in their place! The needs of the learners come first—*all* the learners,' said Julia, with mock severity.

'Yes, ma'am!' Wendy grinned. 'Have you met him yet? I suppose not, being away so long.'

'I wasn't away *that* long,' Julia reminded her gently, thinking of the weeks she had spent nursing her mother after a stroke. She liked to think they were not wasted weeks, even though her mother had suffered a second, fatal, stroke. Now she was alone again, at twenty-six completely alone, without even a distant cousin as far as she knew. 'And no, I haven't met your Dr Paul Konrad, but I've heard about him. He's some kind of tall, dark and handsome wonderman, I hear.'

'That sounds a bit jaundiced!' remonstrated Wendy. 'He isn't that tall and not that handsome, but he's dark,' she added helpfully. 'He's a heart man.'

'That could be useful. The students don't get enough experience in that field,' Julia put in, warming to the new consultant.

'He's wonderful with the patients, but he's a bit testy with us mere nurses,' Wendy went on, and Julia's mental picture of a benign, smiling cardiologist dissolved. 'He's foreign. Got a very sexy accent,' Wendy added, sorting the students' records into neat piles.

'Does he like, merely tolerate, or actively dislike students?' asked Julia, her mind still toying with the idea of enlisting the man's help. 'Even if he thinks he's a cut above us, he may be tolerant towards the youngsters. I might ask him to take some of them on one of his rounds,' she went on, enthusiasm creeping back into her voice as it always did when she was discussing her students and planning new ways of instructing them.

'He tolerates students, from what they tell me, but he's hardly got his foot in the door yet. He's got our beloved Principal Tutor eating out of his hand, though!'

'That must be a sight worth seeing,' Julia said dryly, picturing the stately Miss Smith gazing down adoringly at the dumpy foreign doctor she envisaged.

'Oh, and he's a widower,' Wendy put in, carefully avoiding Julia's gaze. 'I knew there was something else about him. Ideal, rea——' She stopped, flushing.

Julia completed the sentence for her. 'Ideal really, him being a widower and me a widow. We could have cosy evenings by the fire, exchanging hard-luck stories!'

'Oh, Julia, I didn't mean it that way! Or perhaps I did,' her friend admitted. 'It's time you stopped mourning, got out and about and——'

'I do get out and about, and I *have* stopped mourning,' Julia assured her, surprised to find that it was true. She'd had little more than a year of marriage and almost three years of widowhood. Sadly, time was blurring her memories of John, yet it blurred the pain, too. Now it was merely a dull ache, and sometimes a whole day would go by without her thinking of him, dreaming of what might have been. The baby they'd planned to have would be about two now . . .

Deliberately she closed her mind to what might have been. The learners were her children, her future. She loved her work as clinical teacher at St Crispin's, a large, celebrated hospital in the south-east of England. The work gave her contact with patients as well as with learners, and, by teaching, she was passing on some of her own expertise to the new generation. St Crispin's was famed for its progressive attitude towards nurse education and there was a waiting list for places. She hoped Nurse Dalton had been admitted on merit like the other candidates. A small frown marred the smoothness of her wide brow. She would not tolerate passengers amongst the students and would not hesitate to tell Dr Konrad so. Sally Dalton must earn her passage.

'You're wearing your "consultants must be kept in their place" expression again!' laughed Wendy. 'I see

fireworks ahead. He isn't a man to trifle with, Julia.
You've met your match,' she warned. The telephone
rang then and Julia automatically reached for it, pushing
arrogant heart specialists firmly to the back of her mind.
She would do battle with the man, if necessary. Perhaps
Dr Paul Konrad had met *his* match. Time would tell.

Later, she strolled through the corridors of St
Crispin's checking up on the students and pupils already
working on the wards. They had just over one hundred,
though one group was in block at present. When they
were on the wards the Senior Tutor arranged occasional
study days, and they had two-week periods when they
were in school. Otherwise their education was in the
hands of Julia and the other clinical teachers. She preferred working with the learners on the wards and had
no desire to become a tutor, because this would mean
being tied to the school of nursing, not being able to
assess the learners on their work where it mattered—on
the wards. Anyway, she would miss the patients and
the camaraderie she found among ward staff.

She found that Dr Konrad had already made his mark
on the hospital. Sister on Stuart Ward, Female Medical,
spoke highly of him, and she was one of the old school,
not given to praising anyone if she could help it. 'Such a
change!' she said proudly, as if the excellence of the new
consultant was entirely her doing.

Julia made no comment as she followed Sister
Whatley on to the ward, her five foot eight dwarfing the
figure of the grey-haired Ward Sister.

Stuart Ward had thirty beds and was full, as was usual
in late spring. 'There's a waiting list,' Sister said, resigna-
tion in her voice, 'but at least we haven't beds in the aisle
now!'

'Hope we never see another winter like that one. It

made nursing terribly difficult,' Julia agreed. The harsh and prolonged winter had meant that all the medical wards were full—more than full, in fact, because they had to put up extra beds for a time. Even Tudor Ward was reopened for a few weeks but was now closed again because of lack of adequate staffing. Now they were just getting back to normal. Because of an outbreak of Asian 'flu, Julia had been called upon to work on the wards for a time, nurses as well as patients having fallen victim to the illness. Clinical teachers normally worked alongside nurses in training in order to teach a specific procedure or to supervise and assess their work, but during the winter Julia and some of her colleagues had worked full shifts on the medical and geriatric wards. She had found it fulfilling and educational, seeing how trained nurses managed to cope with inadequate resources and too few helpers. During that time she felt the learners had been helped by seeing that teachers could also be 'doers'.

After she had checked on the learners, Julia went up to those patients who were confined to bed and had a word with each. Tomorrow she would start her work in earnest, rolling up the sleeves of her white dress and working alongside her learners. For today she wanted to get her bearings, see what each patient was suffering from, check on the progress of each student and pupil. In addition to her clinical work she had also to supervise the other teachers. She had a team of four, but that wasn't nearly enough. Perhaps the new man might— Irritably she thrust the thought away, annoyed that the new consultant was constantly in her thoughts. She didn't *want* to dwell on the man, wondering if he had an answer for this problem or that one. Because he was a visiting consultant on a two-year contract, any innovations he suggested might be resented. They would be transient, also, most probably leaving when he did. He would be returning to whatever research he was engaged in and St Crispin's would be as before. Yet he sounded the type to bring the wind of change with him, blowing away the cobwebs, the dust, and signalling a new era for the hospital.

I wish he could blow away *my* cobwebs, Julia thought, as she finished her tour, returning to Sister's office for a brief discussion.

Something struck her as she gazed down at her list. On it she had written down each patient's name, diagnosis, probable prognosis and medication. Alongside that was the name of the consultant in charge of that particular patient, and she re-checked their names. Yes, she was right. Not one patient was listed as being under the care of Dr Konrad, and she voiced her surprise to Sister Whatley. Sister beamed. 'That's because he has his own ward! He wanted his patients segregated.'

Surprised, Julia asked: 'Whatever for? We already have cardiac beds and——'

'Because of his research, my dear girl,' Sister explained patiently. 'He isn't touching congestive cardiac failure at all. He's going to treat mainly patients with severe angina, or those who've had minor heart attacks in the past. The research is into ways of combating stress, giving the patients a better quality of life without operations, if possible.'

'Is he going to use them as guinea-pigs?' Julia wondered aloud, and Sister Whatley snorted.

'Of course he isn't! If they need treatment, they will get it. If they need an operation, then they'll go on Mr Almazan's waiting list. No, he believes that if stress levels can be lowered, the patient stands a better chance of making a full recovery.' Julia had never heard her colleague so enthusiastic as she went on: 'Even those who really need a by-pass op can be helped. A spell here beforehand can build up their strength, and he says a relaxing atmosphere in itself can be curative.'

'It sounds good—in principle,' Julia said cautiously. 'Where *is* this new ward? We're having to close beds because of lack of staff and we can't possibly——'

'They've re-opened Tudor Ward again for him! Isn't that good? He certainly gets things done. He's a quick worker!' Sister went on, beaming, and Julia raised her eyebrows.

'I thought there wasn't sufficient staff to keep Tudor open on a permanent basis? We could certainly use those extra beds, but where are the nurses coming from?'

She managed to hide her enthusiasm so thoroughly that Sister Whatley frowned. 'I thought you would be pleased, Julia! Anyway, the nursing quota has been increased. Dr Konrad must have leaned on someone important,' she went on. 'It's only a small ward, as you know. It will be mixed, I'm afraid.' Here her tone became disapproving, and Julia hid a smile. Mixed wards were unacceptable to the older staff.

Dr Konrad was, it transpired, working in an advisory capacity until his own ward was ready. 'He will also be helping out on Brer Rabbit, I expect.'

Brer Rabbit was the children's ward and Julia intended going there next. She rose and thanked her older colleague for the tea. 'I must rush around now. This is my first call,' she smiled. 'By the time I finish I shall be awash with tea!'

Sister grunted. 'It's a good job nurses have enormous bladders! Oh . . .' She paused, then went on: 'You haven't met him yet, have you?'

'Who? Dr Konrad? No, not yet. This *is* my first day back,' Julia pointed out. She was keen to meet the man, particularly now. If he had the influence to get a closed ward re-opened then he could be of use to her for her learners, and she said as much to Sister Whatley. Although so different in age, they had known each other since Julia had arrived at the hospital as a raw eighteen-year-old. Sister Whatley was in charge of the ward on which Julia had started her training and she had great respect for the woman's clinical expertise.

Sister pursed her lips, her expression shrewd as she met Julia's gaze. 'He might be of use to you in other ways, young woman. Time you stopped grieving and settled down. If I was twenty years younger I'd make a grab for him myself! Now off with you, I'm too busy to sit gossiping!' she added, before Julia could react to the personal remark.

Stop grieving and settle down indeed! She was quietly fuming as she hastily toured the other training wards. First Wendy, now Sister Whatley! How dared they! Didn't they realise that after John there would be no one for her? Sister Whatley, in particular, ought to know that. It was through her she had met John, who was a newly-qualified staff nurse on the ward Sister was then running. He had helped her a lot with her studies and she sailed through her Finals at the first attempt, collecting the hospital's Gold Medal on the way. Both of them loved nursing and felt that the patient was the most important person on the ward. Do I still believe that? Julia asked herself sadly, as she made her lonely way across the car park towards the School of Nursing. Somehow, after John's tragic death, her idealism had vanished. She was a good nurse, no more than that.

Life was unfair. Why couldn't they both have been

killed in that horrific rail crash? Instead, although many passengers were injured, the only fatality was her beloved John, Julia herself escaping without a scratch. Physically she was unmarked, but no one knew how deep the mental scars went. She had loved and lost. By loving you eventually got hurt, so . . . no more loving, she told herself firmly, as she waved to one of the doctors who had asked her out a few times before giving up hope. No more loving, therefore no more heartache: it was a simple equation. Sister Whatley could keep her well-meant advice. Dr Paul Konrad was in no danger from *this* nurse!

By the end of the week Julia had heard so much about Dr Konrad that she began to get cross. 'He seems to be a wonderman! Superman plus plus!' she complained to Wendy on Friday afternoon. 'He's elusive. I haven't managed to track him down yet, but he's getting on my nerves already.'

Wendy's eyes twinkled. 'Wait until you meet him! Perhaps we'll see something of him in the School when the new set start on Monday.'

Julia had half forgotten Sally Dalton, who was the daughter of Dr Konrad's girl-friend, if rumour was to be believed. 'If he interferes with Nurse Dalton's education I shall show him the door,' she said firmly, 'superman or no superman!'

'Mrs Dalton used to be a model—one of those tall, willowy creatures. The kind I envy,' Wendy sighed. 'I met her when Sally came for interview. You must have been away that day—oh yes, you were at that conference. Sally's built like a fashion model, too, from what I remember.'

Julia sighed. 'I know modelling isn't the easy work it

seems to us, but nursing is a great deal harder. Never mind,' she went on briskly, 'perhaps Dr Konrad will motivate the girl. He may not be such a burden to us after all!'

'I hope you will not find me a burden, Sister.'

Julia whirled round, her eyes widening as they rested on the figure in the doorway.

Wendy recovered first, and hastily introduced them. Julia grasped the large hand held out to her and even managed a shaky smile as she came face-to-face at last with Dr Paul Konrad.

Grave dark eyes swept over her, yet there was nothing sensual in his appraisal of the tall, slender red-haired Sister. It was more a cold, clinical assessment of a patient, and perversely she resented it.

Wendy's description of the consultant as 'not that tall and not that handsome' must have been Wendy in a mischievous playful mood, for Paul Konrad was both tall and good-looking. Perhaps he wasn't handsome in the Hollywood superstar mould, and his strongly defined features and firm jaw were touched with ruthlessness, yet it was a face Julia found attractive, even compelling. Those deep-set eyes held hers for a moment, then he permitted himself the faintest of smiles. The smile did not reach his eyes, and a little shiver of apprehension shot through her.

She wondered whether to apologise for her remark about him being a burden, then decided against it. They would be crossing swords quite a bit in the future, she felt sure. Wendy's words about Julia meeting her match might have been prophetic, for clearly he would be a hard man to cross. Her lips curved into a warm smile and, despite her apprehension, she found herself looking forward to the battle.

CHAPTER TWO

'There will be twelve beds only—enough, I think.' The tall, powerfully-built consultant raised a brow as if inviting Julia to comment, and she found herself agreeing that twelve beds would certainly be enough.

They were on Tudor Ward, a ward empty of patients as yet, but the beds were already in place in two-bedded cubicles, the cupboards full of linen, equipment ready, even trained nurses lined up.

'There will be two nurses coming from an agency,' Dr Konrad went on, the deep voice with its slight foreign inflection doing strange things to Julia's hearing. The voice seemed to be inside her, part of her. She heard the words echoing in her head almost as if she was speaking them. Hastily she pulled herself together as liquid brown eyes homed in on her.

'What about the other staff?' she queried, fiddling awkwardly with the cuffs of her crisp white uniform dress. They stood on opposite sides of the last bed in the ward, just as they would if they were consultant and Ward Sister doing a round of the patients.

He shrugged broad shoulders. 'They will come from other wards, wherever they can be spared. I want experienced nurses only,' he added.

Julia's eyes widened. 'But you must have students!' she protested hotly. She had been mentally making plans, juggling with faces and names in her head as she sought for suitable senior learners to send him. 'It will be a splendid training opportunity for them,' she went on,

15

as the consultant surveyed her in silence, his heavy-lidded eyes dark and unfathomable.

'It would be a unique experience,' he agreed at last. 'However, I have decided against beginners. I must have trained staff only.' Purposefully he strode away, leaving her speechless with fury. The war had begun already, but he need not think he'd won the first battle. If he thought that, he didn't understand Sister Julia Carr!

She made her leisurely way back to the ward office. Leisurely, because she wanted to avoid any suggestion that she was desperate to catch him up, to argue the case for her student nurses. Let him think she had capitulated already. That way he would be caught off guard when she launched her offensive!

She smiled pleasantly at him as she reached the empty office. He was leaning against the desk, arms folded, a cynical smile hovering about his wide mouth. It was a hard mouth, she decided, only the full lower lip conveying the merest hint of sensuality. Again the aura of ruthlessness struck her, and her resolution faltered for an instant.

She mustn't let her imagination run away with her. The man was a doctor, for heaven's sake! He wasn't a bandit chief or a terrorist ready to kill for some mistaken ideal. Yet he worried her.

'You have hoisted the battle standard, Sister Carr.' It was a statement rather than a question, and she flushed at the shrewdness of his remark.

She had the clear, translucent skin of the true redhead, and there was no way she could halt the tide of colour that swept over her face. Embarrassed, she let the anger show in her expression.

'Your eyes are the colour of the sea on a hot summer's

day; deep, deep blue,' he murmured as she struggled to control her anger. He was the absolute limit!

'Thank you, sir,' she managed. The colour faded, leaving her pale, accentuating the vivid blueness of her eyes and the soft pink of her mouth. She felt vulnerable, horribly vulnerable, in this man's presence, and she resented it. He had no right to make her feel young and desirable again, yet that was the effect he had on her. 'If you'll excuse me, I have to get back to the School.' This time she had her emotions under their usual tight control, and the smile she turned on the heart specialist was cool and businesslike.

He nodded. 'I will walk back with you.' That was the last thing she wanted, but she could hardly say so. Instead she drew her cloak around her like a shell as they strolled from the main hospital towards the School of Nursing. Julia cast a glance at the consultant as he walked by her side. He was a large man and made even her feel small and dainty. Although she was slender, her height meant she stood head and shoulders above most of her female colleagues. Even the male ones were often at eyeball level with her, and it was comforting to find a man she had to look up to.

They parted at the door of the School, the consultant leaving her with an urbane smile. Julia's eyes followed him and she despised herself for that weakness. She had no interest in the man whatever and she was behaving like a gauche schoolgirl.

She noted with surprise that it was well past five. Going home time already, and she hadn't nearly finished all the paperwork she wanted to clear before the weekend. 'Damn the man!' she said aloud. If he hadn't invited her over to Tudor she could have been on her way home by now. Yet home was an empty, cheerless flat she rented in the nearby town of Kessett, and she was in no hurry. She could not blame the consultant for keeping her, anyway. It wasn't as if he'd *ordered* her to inspect Tudor Ward! It must have been a polite gesture from a visiting doctor to a Senior Sister, nothing more than that. And medical nursing had once been her chosen speciality. Perhaps Sister Whatley had mentioned her interest in cardiac nursing.

She spent Saturday morning in Brighton, lunching there with Wendy and her husband who were on a shopping spree, then, on impulse, she turned her car towards the hills.

She parked in a small car park near the Downs. There were only one or two cars there as it was rather early in the season for visitors. She and John had often walked across the South Downs. Rambling was one of his hobbies which he had shared with her. Now, whenever her problems boiled over or she felt particularly blue, she turned to the ancient ways of the hills for comfort. At least now she didn't have to hurry back because her mother fretted when she was out.

John at least would approve, she mused as she trod the familiar paths. She decided she could comfortably manage two miles or so. Often they had walked to Birling Gap, but that was a much greater distance than she could cope with alone. Distances seemed shorter when one had a companion. Tears pricked her eyelids and she stopped to wipe away a tear which struggled free and was making its slow but sure way down her delicately-flushed cheek. The wind was keener than she had anticipated and she longed for her fleecy-lined anorak instead of the spring jacket she wore. Her red-gold hair tumbled about her in the wind and she struggled to tie the headscarf she'd brought, then gave it up as a bad job.

With her vision obscured by wayward strands of hair, she did not see the trio until she was nearly upon them. When she realised, she paused, half inclined to flight, but it was too late. There was no polite way she could turn back now. Certainly she could not pretend she hadn't seen Dr Konrad and his two female companions. Three pairs of dark eyes were turned towards her, and she smiled uncertainly, not sure of her reception.

'Good afternoon, Dr Konrad,' she said quietly. 'I didn't know you enjoyed walking, too.'

'I have few hobbies, but I need the exercise,' he answered politely, then, reluctantly it seemed, introduced the women. One was her new student, Sally Dalton; the other was Sally's mother, Rowena. Sally's smile was shy yet warm, and Julia took to her immediately. She was a tall rather gangling teenager, rather as Julia herself had once been. Her long dark hair was tied back neatly with a long white silk scarf, making Julia feel untidier than ever. She was rather annoyed that one of her learners had caught her off balance.

Mrs Dalton was even taller than Julia, and slim as far as one could judge. She was snuggled into an anorak on top of a vivid scarlet trouser suit. Her glossy black hair was unruffled by the wind and must have been heavily lacquered. Her dark eyes, so like those of Dr Konrad, made a swift appraisal of Julia. Apparently she decided Julia was harmless, and bestowed a charming smile upon her. 'You will be in charge of my daughter, I believe?' Her voice was soft and beautifully modulated, and the hand she held out to Julia was soft, too, white with long silver-tipped nails. The hand of a woman who did no housework nor such mundane nursing chores as bed-bathing and back rounds!

'The Senior Tutor is in charge of the learners while

they're in study block,' Julia explained, while Sally listened intently. 'On the ward each learner is under the care of one of our clinical teachers, and I'm in overall charge of them. I also teach on the wards, practical procedures like medicine rounds, giving injections, bed——'

'I don't think I could bear to give an injection!' Sally interrupted, and Julia smiled understandingly. She knew the feeling only too well.

'It comes with practice, Nurse Dalton,' she assured the girl, watching as Sally blushed at being addressed as 'Nurse'.

'Nurse Dalton already!' Dr Konrad put in gently. 'See, you have begun your career, my child!'

Consultant and student smiled at each other, and Julia felt excluded. So, apparently, did Mrs Dalton, for she put a proprietorial hand on his arm. 'We mustn't keep Mrs Carr, darling. She sees plenty of doctors and nurses when she's at the hospital! Isn't that right?' She appealed to Julia to back her up.

Julia saw the doctor glance at her wedding ring when Mrs Dalton called her 'Mrs'. He must have thought her single before, for she never wore her ring on duty. Her name-badge described her simply as 'J. Carr, Senior Clinical Teacher'. 'That's the truth,' she agreed lightly. 'I'll see you some time on Monday, Nurse,' she told Sally, then murmured a polite goodbye before continuing her solitary walk.

Although the footpath led upwards the incline was gentle. It would have been a pretty walk if it wasn't for the wind. Julia paused once she was out of the consultant's sight, to take her bearings. She was some distance from the sea and believed that once she was at the top of the slope she would see the small Downland villages spread out before her. She hadn't made this particular journey for some years and was afraid of getting lost, yet she couldn't turn back now. She wanted to give Dr Konrad and the women time to retrace their steps. They had obviously been picnicking, having found shelter from the wind behind a rock escarpment and a clump of bushes already bursting with flowers.

Sally and the doctor seemed close, and Julia pondered on that as she made her slow way against the wind. Could he be the girl's father? she wondered. He was about the right age and must be well into his thirties. The crisp black hair was faintly flecked with grey, with just a touch at the temples. Enough to give him a distinguished look.

She was panting by the time she reached the top, but the view made it all worthwhile. Far in the distance she saw a dolls'-house-size village nestling in the valley, while nearer at hand the river Ouse wound torturously through the landscape. Despite the wind, she stood for several minutes breathing in the tranquil scene. It was on a Sunday that she and her husband had last followed this footpath. Far away, carried on the wind, she thought she heard church bells, just as on that Sunday long ago. It must be a trick of the wind. Disappointment flooded through her—disappointment and yearning for what was and could never be again. She tried to conjure up John's face and voice, his special smile meant for her alone, but the distance in time was too great. All she could hear was the church bells, all she could see was the dark, unfathomable eyes of Paul Konrad.

Choking on a sob, she turned and almost ran down the path, eager to escape from her tormentor. He was probably back in Kessett by now. He had no right to torment her imagination like this. She cried as she ran, thankful that no one could see her. As a senior teacher, she had a certain reputation to maintain. She was already regarded as aloof and untouchable by the male staff, a charge which was all too true. She could not afford human feelings except where her students and the patients were concerned. Her own needs and unhappiness she must keep locked within her. If you loved you got hurt: that was the maxim which she must keep for ever before her, and she resented Dr Konrad's intrusion into her life. How dared he tell her that her eyes were blue like the sea! It was a meaningless, flowery phrase and he would do better to keep it for Rowena Dalton. All she wanted from him was his clinical expertise and an interest in her students.

When she reached the part of the Downs where she had met the consultant she hesitated, but need not have worried. All trace of their picnic had gone. Loneliness hit her, shocking her by its intensity. Feeling foolish, she gazed around, as if she could conjure up the doctor or some trace of his passing, but there was nothing. Then her eyes caught a gleam of white. Moving nearer, she saw that it was a white scarf, the one Sally Dalton had worn. She must have let her hair loose and then forgotten the scarf when they moved off. It was snagged, and Julia had difficulty in prising it from the rock where it must have been swept by the wind. She didn't want to damage the delicate fabric more than it had been already. It was real silk and smelled of a delicate citrus scent.

Tying her own headscarf firmly to keep out the wind, she folded Sally's and put it in her bag. The thought struck her that they might return for it, but she didn't want to take the risk. The capricious wind might hurl it on to the gorse.

If she toyed with the idea that the doctor himself might return, she was disappointed. She reached her car without encountering another soul. Cross with herself for even *wanting* to see the wretched man again, she unlocked the door, then heard a voice calling. Startled out of her reverie, she could not at first see anyone, but she was looking for an adult. The person calling her was a small girl of about nine or so. The child waved vigorously, and Julia paused, wondering if someone needed first aid. She reached into the car for her first aid kit, then relocked the car door as the child approached.

'Please, I'm looking for Suki! Have you seen her? And Tim, too,' she added as an afterthought.

'Are Suki and Tim your dogs?' Julia asked gently. 'Perhaps they're chasing rabbits. They can probably hear you but don't want to come yet.'

'No!' the girl said crossly. 'Suki's my dog. Tim's my baby brother.' She ran off, and a bemused Julia followed. She might need the first aid kit after all.

They kept calling the dog's name and once or twice Julia called to the boy. According to the girl, Tess Plummer, Tim was nearly three. Their parents were separated and they lived with their mother.

'Did you come up here on your own?'

Tess nodded. 'I told Mum, but she didn't say we couldn't. I don't think she's very well, but I made her a cup of tea,' she went on, matter-of-factly. She appeared to have no fear of strangers and put her hand trustingly in Julia's as they carefully searched the Downs. Eventually their efforts were rewarded as a huge black and white dog came bounding towards them. Tess fell upon it with cries of delight, and dog and child were a mass of arms, legs and fur as they greeted each other.

'We must find Tim,' Julia reminded her after the first

greetings were over. Suki stood on her hind legs and
tried to lick Julia's face, then bounded off.

'Suki!' screeched Tess. 'Wait!'

The dog stopped some distance away, barking, then
ran off, pursued by Julia and Tess. It did this several
times and obviously knew where it was going. Julia's
fears for the boy multiplied. He might be lying dead
somewhere. Perhaps he'd fallen down a ledge or broken
his leg. Anything could have happened to him, and
she held Tess's hand tightly, preventing the girl from
galloping away and injuring herself as well.

They heard Tim's crying before they saw him. The
small, jean-clad figure was sitting against a bush with
tears tumbling down his face.

'Stop crying!' his sister said crossly. 'You're a big boy
now.' Despite her concern over the boy, Julia couldn't
fail to be amused by the girl's 'little mother' attitude.
Tess cuddled him against her, making soothing noises
just as she must have seen her mother do.

After she had been introduced as 'a kind nurse to
make you better' Julia was able to examine him. His
tears dried once he saw his rescuers, but agony showed
in his eyes, and he was deathly pale. He had been
throwing a ball for Suki and tripped. His leg hurt, he told
Julia, but it was the pain in his arm she was more worried
about. He screamed as she touched it, even though she
was gentle. He had probably fallen on his outstretched
arm and she thought he had fractured his clavicle in his
fall. He was supporting his right arm in a characteristic
way, inclining his head towards the injured side. Speaking soothingly, she examined his legs as far as was
possible through the jeans but couldn't locate a fracture
there. Tim didn't want her to touch his right knee, and it
felt swollen. It was possible he'd sprained it, perhaps

landing with it under him as he fell.

Swiftly she did the best she could with the limited equipment available. She didn't want to remove his jeans for a closer inspection in case she chilled him. The main problem was to immobilise his arm and shoulder, then somehow manage to carry him down to the car, which was some distance away now. He looked a heavy child and, in the wind, it would be no easy task. She couldn't ask Tess to go for help. There was a phone-box within a couple of miles, but it was too risky sending the child. The mother had no business letting two young children loose on the Downs, anyway, and Julia did not intend to compound the error. They would have to manage somehow. Once in the car she would drive to St Crispin's, then get a message to Mrs Plummer somehow.

Removing the boy's sweater was no easy matter, and he began to cry again. She dived into her first aid kit for the triangular bandages, then made up a sling as a very temporary measure, placing another bandage folded up as a pad around his neck. Ideally, his shoulders should be braced back with the aid of two triangular bandages, but she hesitated to hurt him further. If he wasn't jolted, the sling would help until they reached Casualty.

Praying that they would meet help on the way down but doubting it, she began her descent with the boy cradled against her. At first she had decided he might walk. When she stood him gingerly on his feet he seemed all right and, encouraged by his sister, he took a few steps, then cried to be picked up because his knee hurt. So it was with the child clinging to her that Julia moved off, preceded by Tess and the dog. Tim was crying again before they'd gone a hundred yards, then the dog barked and went bounding ahead. A man was coming towards them, and Julia wondered if it might be the children's father. Then as the dog sniffed warily at his hand she saw it was Paul Konrad.

Relief shot through her, coupled with an idiotic pleasure at seeing him again. He must have returned to search for Sally's scarf. 'Thank goodness!' she cried, setting down her whimpering burden as he hurried towards them followed by the huge dog.

The consultant's dark eyes narrowed at her enthusiastic welcome, then he quickly sized up the situation. Feeling foolish at greeting him so warmly, Julia put him in the picture, then knelt by his side as he gently probed the boy's injuries. He sent Tess down to his own car, which was nearer than Julia's, placing his car keys in her small hand and asking her to fetch a blanket and his black bag.

'Be a good boy, Tim, and let me look at your poor knee and arm. Hm?' Tim gazed up trustingly, all traces of tears vanishing, and Julia felt a warm glow at the compassionate way the doctor tended to the child. Strong yet gentle hands probed and examined. The knee was swollen but it didn't seem that bad. Probably rest and cold water compresses would cure that.

'The clavicle is fractured, as you say,' he murmured, his touch drawing a small yelp of protest from Tim. His arm accidentally brushed against Julia's and she tensed, wishing *she* could yelp in protest! She berated herself for her stupidity, but the doctor seemed not to notice her instinctive movement away from him.

Tess, panting, came up with the required items, the consultant performed the first aid treatment Julia had been reluctant to try, and soon they were on their way down again. This time Dr Konrad carried the boy while Julia walked behind with Tess and the doctor's bag.

In no time at all they were in Casualty at St Crispin's.

During the drive Julia supported the child on her lap, sitting in the back of the car beside Tess, the dog sprawling in an untidy heap at their feet. Although the first aid had eased the boy's damaged arm he was in much pain, and Julia was glad to hand him over to Sister Casualty.

Julia offered to wait until the child's injuries were assessed and treated more fully, though there wasn't much more than could be done for a broken collarbone. Then she remembered that her car was still on the Downs. She could not have driven to the hospital in her own car because she was needed to tend the child during the journey; they could hardly have left that to Tess. As it was she hesitated to mention the matter to the consultant. She would get a taxi, drop the children off at their home, then ask the driver to take her to her car. Having come to the decision and considered it to be a sensible one, she was irked when Dr Konrad offered her a lift to where she had left the car.

'There's no need, really, Doctor. I shall take a taxi,' she said briskly. 'I'll see the children safely in, then carry on up to the Downs. Oh!'—she suddenly remembered the scarf—'Here. This belongs to Nurse Dalton.' She handed him the scarf and he stared at it. 'That was what you returned for, wasn't it?' she went on.

Dark eyes met hers and she felt uncomfortable under his scrutiny, so much so that she babbled on: 'The scarf—it belongs to Nurse Dalton, I think. I found it near where you were picnicking. It . . . it caught on a rock. I . . .' She heard herself prattling on, and stopped, mortified. He would think her a complete fool! Not that his opinion mattered all that much. In fact, it mattered not at all.

'So! Nurse Dalton's scarf. I forgot.' Smiling a little, he

put it in his anorak pocket. 'She asked me to search for it while I was up there,' he explained to a puzzled Julia.

'I thought that was the reason you came back? Nurse missed her scarf and you offered to search for it.' Her voice was a little breathless because of the way the consultant was surveying her.

'No. I returned to see if you were all right, Sister Carr.' He eyed her shrewdly. 'You seemed—pale and lost, somehow. I wanted to be sure you were all right. The scarf wasn't of great importance.'

'Oh! I . . .' She stopped, not quite sure what to say. The senior consultant, a newcomer and a foreigner, who must have known she resented him, had gone all the way back just to make sure she was safe!

Her eyes deepened to almost sapphire as he watched with apparent interest. She flushed under his scrutiny, but this time she didn't resent it. Ruthless and arrogant he might be, but there was a softer side to his complex nature, and she had just been given a privileged glimpse of it. He was so unlike any of the other men she knew that she was perplexed.

'You blush prettily, Sister,' he said gravely. A smile lurked in the dark, beautiful depths of his eyes, and she found herself at a loss for words.

Despite her protests, he gave her a lift back to the Downs to collect her car, once they had taken the children home. Mrs Plummer was overjoyed to see the children back, and took Julia's advice to heart not to let them wander over the Downs again.

To Julia's surprise the drive back to the Downs passed pleasantly enough. At Dr Konrad's request she pointed out various landmarks, including the famous Long Man of Wilmington, an ancient giant etched on the hills.

'I must see what I can while I'm here,' he commented

as he set her down opposite her small car. His was a sleek silver Mercedes and dwarfed her own. When she asked where he came from, he hesitated fractionally, then shrugged. 'I call myself the doctor from nowhere,' he said quietly. 'I'm a British subject, but I've been lecturing on heart disease in the USA. When I complete my two years at St Crispin's I shall return there for a while.'

His accent suggested that he hadn't been British all that long, but since he evidently did not want to talk about the more distant past, Julia had to be content.

As she drove slowly back to Kessett, she found herself dwelling upon the enigmatic Dr Konrad. He intrigued her. There was an aura of power about him that she found compelling. It was all rather disturbing, and she had to make a conscious effort to put him from her mind.

CHAPTER THREE

THE following week was so busy that Julia had no time to dwell upon her feelings for the enigmatic doctor.

Perhaps that was as well, she thought, as she took a small party of students to Stuart Ward on Wednesday. It was the new set, four out of the fifteen who had started two days before—all girls this time. The group she had in tow included Sally Dalton, who was something of a puzzle. She was intelligent, highly so, Julia judged, and she had no difficulty in understanding instructions. In fact, she was already beginning to help the others. Yet something was lacking—the urge to nurse, perhaps. Without that she would not get far. The sheer hard grind of ward work was offputting to all but the very keen. She was pleasant and helpful to patients, though, and it could be that she needed time to settle.

Sister Whatley beamed at them. The four had already visited Stuart Ward with other clinical teachers but had stayed only one hour. Most of their early work would be done in school. Apart from lectures from the teaching staff, various doctors gave talks on diverse subjects. In addition, certain practical procedures were best learned in the school's practical room. Important though all this was, patient contact was just as important, and right from the first day the set had been introduced to real ward work.

'What are you nurses going to do for me this morning?' asked Sister Whatley, but before Julia could reply, Sally Dalton's quiet voice said: 'Hello, Uncle Paul.'

Startled, both Sisters turned to face the consultant. 'Good morning, Dr Konrad,' Julia said politely, 'I hope I'm not disturbing you?'

Paul Konrad considered her for a brief moment, and she averted her gaze, fearing that his scrutiny might cause her to blush in front of the learners. 'Perhaps just a little,' he suggested, and she bit her lip savagely, unsure of his meaning. 'I thought you might like to visit Tudor when your young ladies are fully occupied.'

Surprised, she readily took up his suggestion. Staff Nurse volunteered to take over the instruction on the making of occupied beds, so Julia felt able to leave the group for a short while. She indicated to them the rest of the beds she wanted remade, then joined Dr Konrad. Her face was flushed from the exercise, and he smiled.

'You are out of condition, Sister Carr. Or should I call you Mrs Carr?' His eyes held an unspoken question, and Julia hesitated before replying frankly that she was a widow.

'I'm usually called Sister by the learners, but properly, clinical teachers and tutors are called Miss or Mrs,' she explained.

He was so close as they walked through to Tudor that she could breathe in the subtle scent of his aftershave. This was combined with the smell of good tweed. His jacket was a subdued lovat tweed which he wore with beautifully-creased cords and a cream shirt and tie. Highly polished shoes completed the ensemble. Julia was used to consultants appearing on the wards in sober grey suits, but she had to admit she liked his outfit, particularly the jacket. John had preferred tweed and for his last birthday she had bought him a dark tweed jacket—the one he was wearing when he died.

Momentarily she shut her eyes, remembrance of that day, that jacket, more than she could bear.

'Sister Carr? Are you unwell?' The deep voice sounded concerned, and her eyes shot open.

She felt guilty at being caught indulging in personal memories during working hours. 'I'm fine, really, Doctor.' Her smile was bright as she tried to reassure him, but she could not hide the pain in her eyes.

He nodded as if satisfied, then proudly ushered her into his portion of the cardiac unit. Her eyes widened. There had been some changes since the previous Friday. The number of beds had dropped, for one thing, and she turned to him, puzzled. 'What happened to your twelve beds?'

'I decided to cut down. It was too crowded—see.' He pointed to a large plan of the ward spread out on a table in the office. Julia smiled at Sister Linda Greene, who was in charge of the newly-opened ward. Sister Greene, a dainty blonde of about thirty, returned the smile warily, perhaps thinking that Julia was bringing some learners to upset the routine.

'Sister Carr has expressed interest in seeing our new ward,' the consultant said smoothly, as if aware of the coolness between the two.

Linda Greene was an efficient, hard-working member of staff, but not a happy one. Her marriage was uninteresting and her husband irritated her; she had said so often enough. As Julia crossed over to the side table to stand beside the consultant she could feel Linda's eyes boring into their backs. Sister Whatley said everyone was falling for the new man, and she appeared to be right. Everyone except Sister Julia Carr, of course.

'Here, this is the main area.' Dr Konrad pointed to the plan. 'We have our beds in cubicles of two, as you saw last week, but more room was needed for relaxation, so there are ten beds only.' He glanced down at her as she tried to work out for herself why relaxation should need so much space. She didn't want to show her ignorance by asking too many questions, not in front of Linda, anyway.

'The relaxation area,' she began, 'I'm not quite sure why you needed to move beds.'

'Really, Julia!' Linda's silky voice broke in on the conversation. 'Surely you read the nursing press?'

Julia swallowed her unwarranted dislike of the other woman. 'Of course,' she murmured, biting her tongue to prevent a more spirited answer. She would not lower herself to bitch with the woman.

'Perhaps you are not fully acquainted with the research, Sister Carr,' the consultant put in gently. 'Here.' He handed her a copy of a prominent medical publication. 'There is an article in it detailing some research I carried out in the United States. Read it when you have time. On Tudor Ward we hope to carry out more of what is termed "preventive" medicine,' he went on. 'There isn't enough research into alternative ways of treating coronary disease, so that is why I am here. I want to study the effects of stress, particularly. I am funded for two years only, so we must make progress in that time.'

'Such a short time,' she commented. 'What do you hope to achieve in two years?' She met the cardiologist's gaze, and a sad smile tugged at the corners of his wide mouth. It was a beautiful mouth, she thought foolishly, before accepting his abrupt invitation to meet the patients for herself.

Heedless of her group of students, who were probably finished by now, she willingly allowed herself to be sidetracked. Cardiac medicine and surgery had always fascinated her, and Dr Konrad's research project promised to be all-absorbing. She must try to persuade him to take a senior student, even if only for a week or two. The thought crossed her mind that she would then have an excuse for regular visits to Tudor Ward, and hastily she brushed it aside. She had more than enough tasks without adding another ward to the schedule.

There were ten beds, as Dr Konrad had pointed out, but only five were so far occupied, four of them by men, as she would have expected. The doctor led her to the cubicle where the lone woman reigned in state.

'This is Sister Carr, who is responsible for training the nurses of the future,' he announced. 'Mrs Hammond runs her own business but has come to spend a little while with us,' he explained.

Julia smiled encouragingly at the woman, who managed only a wan half-smile in return. 'I'm here for a rest—or so they tell me,' she whispered as Julia's own warm hand covered the cold one.

'Mrs Hammond came to us yesterday and already is on the mend,' Dr Konrad pronounced.

'If Doctor says I'm on the mend, I must be,' the patient agreed, her pale eyes on the consultant. 'I wouldn't presume to disagree with him.'

Julia, glancing sideways at him, inclined to Mrs Hammond's view. Not many people *would* presume to disagree with the consultant, she reflected. He was a hard man, and she was afraid of losing the battles they must inevitably fight.

They moved on to the other cubicles. Only one man was in bed, and he was asleep. 'He was referred to me by Mr Almazan,' Dr Konrad told her. Mr Almazan was the consultant heart surgeon at St Crispin's. 'The patient asked for surgery, but Mr Almazan felt that he was a patient we could help. We hope to avoid surgery altogether for him, but for some it will still be necessary.'

'And this article you've written, does it explain the project in detail? Set out what you're trying to achieve?' Julia wanted to know.

'Yes. You will find the answers to all your questions there,' he said firmly. 'But see for yourself,' he added, leaving the ward area and preceding her through an archway. 'I have been given two more rooms as well as Tudor Ward.'

'Is that for the relaxation Sister Greene mentioned?'

'Yes, but also for other activities. Our co-ordinator is Sister Greene. She has been of enormous help—a very friendly lady,' he added, a glint of humour in his eyes.

Julia's lips twitched as she struggled not to laugh, then gave it up, her mouth curving into a smile that lit up her whole face.

He paused, his enigmatic gaze on her mouth. 'You should smile more often,' he commented, and she felt the colour leap into her face. Fortunately, his attention was diverted by a houseman, and she was able to escape into the suite of rooms.

Nell, one of their occupational therapists, waved to her as she ventured into the first room. Nell was sitting by a patient, emphasising a point as she walked. Julia half expected to find the men doing basketry or at least some other task to keep them occupied, yet the patient was seated in a comfortable armchair just listening to the therapist. Intrigued, she moved nearer.

Nell beckoned to her, then made the introductions. 'Mr Abbott will be undergoing surgery, Julia, but he's come to Dr Konrad first for assessment,' the occupational therapist explained.

Julia didn't see what assessment the cardiac unit could

provide. She despised herself for her ignorance, and determined to read Dr Konrad's article the first chance she got, perhaps in her lunch break. Mr Abbott was a large man, several stones overweight, with the reddish mottled skin and high colour of the hypertensive.

Another patient, a much taller and fitter-looking man, was watching television in a corner of the room. Not liking to disturb him, Julia crept through to the next room where a number of women were sitting at a table, apparently planning something. She recognised one as a voluntary visitor who came regularly to the medical wards. She paused uncertainly, then sensed the consultant's presence. With some men their aftershave preceded them, but the one he was wearing today was too subtle for that—subtle and elusive, like the man who wore it.

The women greeted him effusively, and Julia suppressed a smile. It was a wonder that such popularity didn't make him swollen-headed. Yet as he talked and made brief introductions, she realised that it wasn't popularity as such. It was greater than that. It was respect and awe for an eminent doctor, and Julia began to realise just how important Dr Paul Konrad and his research were for the future treatment of heart conditions.

The group comprised voluntary visitors, occupational therapy aides, and a psychologist, and Julia became even more intrigued. Paul Konrad explained to her that, in combating stress, various therapies were used. 'Relaxation is very important,' he emphasised. 'Some people cannot relax and need assistance. We provide relaxation sessions to soothing music, gently graded exercises, massage, psychological counselling. Sometimes it is enough that the patient has someone who is prepared to sit and listen to his problems. Often at home there is no one like that. The family may be partly the cause of the patient's problem,' he added.

She found it fascinating and was keen to learn more of the work and how it could benefit cardiac patients, but there were her students to be considered.

Reluctantly she left with the consultant, then raised a finely-arched brow because Sister Greene was hovering in the doorway, with eyes only for Dr Konrad. With a murmured word of thanks to them both, Julia left, hurrying to gather her brood. She had neglected them far too long, but she could not have turned down the chance to see Tudor now it was opened. She clutched the journal to her as she rejoined the students. Reading that was first priority as soon as she had a few minutes free.

She was so busy afterwards that it was lunchtime before she knew it. Lunch was to be a salad in the canteen. She collected her plate of cheese, finely grated raw vegetables and a tomato, then joined the queue to pay. As luck would have it, Linda Greene was just in front of her and it was natural for the two of them to sit together. It was a table for four near the double glass doors which led on to a small terrace. Staff could dine out there in warmer weather, but now it was raining, and Linda eyed the weather gloomily.

'We were going for a stroll this evening, but it looks as if my luck's out,' she said, her direct gaze on Julia as they began their meal.

An arrow hit Julia's heart, then bounced off, and it was a moment before she could speak. 'It's a shame,' she remarked, cutting carefully into the tomato.

'Yes. Still, he might take me for a drive instead,' Linda continued. 'What you lose on the swings you gain on the roundabouts!' she chuckled, her good humour restored.

Julia didn't feel good-humoured, but she smiled, nevertheless. 'Where will you go?' Deliberately she kept her tone neutral. It was obvious that Linda was talking about Paul Konrad. She would hardly get excited about a drive with her husband; it wasn't that sort of marriage.

Linda shrugged. 'Down to the coast, maybe. There's lots of cosy little bays he hasn't seen. He'll want to pack as much into his time here as possible, won't he?'

Julia agreed that he would. There was silence while they ate their salads, Julia having almost lost her appetite.

'He's got a beautiful car, a Mercedes,' her companion broke the awkward silence, but Julia merely smiled as if she had not the slightest interest in the subject. Then Linda's face changed. She went red, then white as Julia watched in amazement. 'He's coming over! Julia, he's going to sit with us!' she hissed.

Julia moved over to make room for Dr Konrad, who paused at their table before asking politely if he might join them. Linda gave her a pointed look as the consultant moved away to place his empty tray on the rack. 'He'll want to talk to me!' she whispered.

'That's fine by me,' Julia said calmly. 'Good conversation adds immeasurably to the pleasure of a meal.' Sink *that* putt, her eyes challenged Linda Greene, as the tall, dark and handsome doctor sat beside her.

He shared his conversation equally between the two of them, but Julia was content to let most of it wash over her. She liked to listen to his accent. She surveyed him discreetly as he and Linda discussed a lecture he was giving to the medical staff. In profile his face lost that touch of ruthlessness she had noticed before, yet it was a hard face, belonging to a man who knew where he was going in life and who intended to get there. The firm, arrogant jaw was a warning to her: Don't fight me, you can't win! Hastily she finished the now unappetising salad, and rose, eager to get back to the school, to plunge into work, work and yet more work. This man unsettled her. Linda could have him with her blessing.

Dr Konrad also rose, even though he hadn't finished his own meal. There was a hint of amused arrogance in his glance, as if he knew she was trying to escape from him. 'I must get on,' he said. 'I will walk as far as the school with you, Sister.'

Julia could hardly tell him she didn't want his company, because in a way she *did*. It was bitter-sweet. There was, too, just the faintest element of danger in it. That element of risk, of venturing into the unknown, was alluring, as far as Dr Paul Konrad was concerned: risky but alluring!

As she might have expected, Linda Greene hurried to join them, pushing away her untasted coffee, but she was detained by another Ward Sister whose loud, hectoring manner meant that there was no chance of Linda escaping until the other Sister had had her say.

Julia wondered where Dr Konrad was taking Linda tonight. It had stopped raining now, and the sun was already out. A perfect evening for a drive.

'Have you read my article yet, Sister Carr?'

'What? Oh, no, I haven't,' she rushed on. 'I'm going to read it tonight. Do you want it back before then?'

'Take your time. There's no hurry,' he assured her. 'You can return it when you dine with me,' he went on casually, and she halted in her tracks.

'Dine?' she echoed, blue eyes wide with surprise.

'In the sunlight your hair turns to a fiery gold,' he commented, throwing her completely.

'You're very free with your flowery compliments, Doctor,' she said in a reproving tone. Naturally she was flattered, but she supposed he paid women compliments as a matter of course. En masse they became meaningless. It hurt that the pretty phrases meant nothing to him.

He ignored her chilly manner as they halted before the School of Nursing. Warily Julia raised her eyes to his, expecting to see amusement in his expression. Instead, he appeared thoughtful. 'Unfortunately I am not free this evening, but tomorrow perhaps?'

'Tomorrow? Tomorrow for *what*, Dr Konrad?'

'For dinner, naturally. I shall pick you up at seven. Until tomorrow, then.' He smiled his half-smile, then turned to go.

She found her voice at last. 'Just a moment, Doctor! I haven't agreed to have dinner with you!' she protested.

'We could discuss my work. Isn't that of interest to you?' His gaze was reproachful, and Julia felt guilty —and curiously let-down. Of course he wanted to talk about his work. She ought to feel flattered.

'Yes, of course it's of interest,' she assured him. 'I'll read your article in bed, then we can discuss it over dinner tomorrow.'

'I shall think of you reading my article in bed, Sister Carr.' His tone was grave, but the look in his dark eyes sent quivers of desire shooting through her slender frame, and she couldn't escape into the School quickly enough.

Once in the sanctuary of her office, she leant against the door, trying to still the demands of her treacherous body. That look had been unmistakable. He was out for all he could get. Tonight, Sister Greene. Tomorrow, Sister Carr. Who else did he have lined up? she wondered bitterly. She had put him on a pedestal, and that was why it hurt so much. That he was a man, with male appetites, she had conveniently forgotten. She knew she was attractive to men, those not put off by her 'teacher's' manner that she seemed unable to shed off duty. Since John there had been no one. Sex was equated with love, in her view, and she could not casually seek a sex partner the way some of the younger nurses did. After John she wanted no man. At least, that was the way it was until she met the doctor from nowhere. Now, too late, she was beginning to realise that she was a woman and that she still needed love and affection.

'And I have the misfortune to become infatuated with a heartless womaniser!' She whispered the words, but they seemed to echo in the room.

Despite her dismay at discovering Dr Konrad's predatory nature, Julia was looking forward to dining with him. The following evening she took extra pains with her appearance, selecting and discarding several outfits before coming down in favour of the deep blue-green. It wasn't new, but it was one of her favourites and the colour did great things for her hair and complexion. The dress was modest in style and perfectly plain. Its very plainness meant she could wear the pearls which had belonged to her mother. The single strand of real pearls did lots for her morale as well as giving her comfort. Because the evenings were still cool she snuggled into her white fake fur jacket.

Seven o'clock, he had said, but she was ready early. She couldn't think how he knew her address, but he didn't ask where she lived, so someone must have told him. Wendy, perhaps? she wondered, feeling a trifle apprehensive as the time drew nearer. If he *did* expect a passionate interlude on the settee, what ought she to do? Keeping him firmly at arm's length was fine in theory but difficult in practice. Did she *want* to keep him at arm's length, anyway? She ducked that question as her ormolu clock at last chimed the hour. Seven o'clock and no sign of him.

Anxiously, she crossed to the window to keep watch. It was an old house and her flat was on the second floor. She rented it from a local firm who used the house as senior staff accommodation. Julia had once nursed the wife of the firm's chairman while she was agency nursing during a holiday, and had been offered accommodation if ever she needed it. After her husband's death she had sold their house and moved into the trained staff residence at St Crispin's. It wasn't a conspicuous success. She found that she needed to get away from the hospital atmosphere off duty, so she contacted the chairman, Mr Randolph, and was lucky enough to be offered the flat. Once business picked up he might need the accommodation, but nothing had been said so far.

The smallish sitting-room overlooked the front drive. Julia settled herself on the window seat, her eyes on the road. Would he find the flat? she wondered, worry gnawing at her nerves. True, it was situated right in the centre of Kessett, but he was a stranger. She began to wish she had suggested meeting outside the hospital, but then their colleagues might see them and the grapevine would burst a blood-vessel in its eagerness to spread the news—the frosty Sister Carr was actually *dating*! Dating the foreign cardiologist, no less. No, she could not have borne that.

Glancing over at the clock, she saw that it was nearly

ten past. It could be that one of his patients had died. The private lives of doctors were always subject to rearrangement at the last moment.

He arrived a few moments later, and she hastily withdrew from the window, not wanting him to know she had been watching and waiting. She had her pride. She didn't want him in the flat, either, so she hastily slammed the flat door and went down to greet him, the precious article in her bag. They would have plenty to discuss.

The tall, broad-shouldered consultant was in the hall-way when she went down. They eyed each other in silence for a moment, then he bowed slightly. 'I have to apologise, Sister Carr,' he said formally. 'There was a cardiac arrest on Stuart and I happened to be passing at the time.'

'I guessed that you'd had an emergency,' she told him as she settled herself in his car. 'I was afraid it was one of Tudor's patients.'

He slid behind the wheel and set the powerful car in motion before replying. 'None of them are at death's door, I hope. Did you find the article of interest?' he went on as they moved out into the sparse traffic.

'Mm, very interesting.' Her face lit up as she detailed the points on which she wanted clarification. 'I'd no idea your project was so special. It would be a wonderful learning opportunity for one of my third-year students,' she added craftily, and he chuckled. It was a deep, throaty chuckle and he sounded genuinely amused.

He made no comment, however, and she decided to let the idea germinate for a while. She would drop another hint later. There was no harm in trying.

They dined at the Harlequin, a restaurant new to Kessett. As they enjoyed a pre-dinner cocktail in the cosy bar Julia couldn't help wondering whether Sister Greene had been wined and dined in the selfsame restaurant the previous evening. Not that she particularly cared, of course. It was merely idle curiosity, she told herself.

'You were frowning, Sister Carr.'

'Sorry. I was turning over a problem in my mind,' she said swiftly. 'Have you dined here before? I know it hasn't been open long and I've been meaning to try it,' she went on casually.

'I came last week. Almazan decided I needed a good square meal,' he smiled, and she relaxed. Linda Greene hadn't dined here last night. They could have gone back to his home for a meal after their drive. And of course, she reasoned to herself, it wasn't likely he would bring her into the town where they might be seen. She was a married woman and he was a senior consultant with a certain dignity to maintain. However much of a Casanova he was, there were ground rules to the flirtation game and he had to obey them . . .

'Shall we dine?' His voice broke into her thoughts and, flustered, she met his gaze. Amusement lurked in his eyes again, and she averted her face lest he read her mind. He was a remarkably shrewd man and she was afraid of revealing too much.

She glanced about with interest as she sat opposite him. The restaurant was small and intimate. There were one or two empty tables, but as far as she could see, they all bore 'Reserved' signs. 'I should imagine you have to book well in advance,' she remarked guilelessly.

Paul Konrad nodded. 'I booked our table last Saturday.' He sounded smug, and she eyed him in surprise.

'Did you book a table on the offchance that you'd find a dinner partner?' she asked, dryly.

'I am never short of dinner partners, Sister Carr,' he assured her, and she couldn't help smiling. No doubt he spoke the truth. It certainly wasn't likely that he had decided last week that Sister Julia Carr was going to dine with him. Her smile faded as she wondered if the table had been intended for him and Linda Greene. No, she had already discounted that idea, but what about Mrs Dalton? She was supposed to be his lady-love.

She struggled to hide her disappointment at his phil-andering ways as she busied herself with the menu. It wasn't her place to sit in judgment on her colleagues. Hadn't she admitted to herself that she found the man attractive? If she didn't watch out she would be his next victim. She wondered uneasily whether she was on the menu for tonight.

They began with prawn cocktail, one of her favourites, and progressed to Steak Tartare. The consultant seemed content to choose the same dishes as Julia, and she found that rather touching. Conversation was kept to the generalities, and whenever she turned to more personal topics, he quickly diverted her attention. She longed to know more about him, wanted to delve into his past. It wasn't inquisitiveness; she genuinely wanted to find out what made him the kind of man he was—aloof, stern, a little out of reach. Then she remembered that he was a womaniser, and to appear too interested in his private life might suggest that she wanted to offer him some tender loving care.

After an excellent light pudding, they relaxed over their coffee, their conversation turning to medical mat-ters as was inevitable. Surprised that he hadn't men-tioned the article again, she broached the subject. After all, that was why he was treating her to a meal.

'You think the project worthwhile?' he asked, and she nodded enthusiastically.

'What made you choose cardiology?' she asked. 'It isn't always very satisfying, is it? Old people with dickey hearts referred to you when they're often beyond help.'

'I prefer younger patients, obviously. If I can give another twenty or more years of good, healthy life to a patient then I am delighted.' He stirred his coffee thoughtfully, and her glance dropped to his large, strong hands. Capable hands. In them a patient would be safe.

'I chose hearts because my father died from a cardiac arrest when I was just a boy. By the time I got to him he was dead, and there was no sophisticated equipment to bring him back to life.' He shrugged, dark eyes sombre. 'Probably nothing could have saved him, but I always wonder. The world is full of "if onlys", Sister.'

Saddened, Julia agreed. 'I often think "if only" when I recall my husband's death,' she told him, surprising herself at telling a comparative stranger. 'If only the car hadn't let us down we wouldn't have been travelling by rail on that particular day at that particular time.' Encouraged by his sympathetic silence, she described briefly what had happened. 'It was a long time before I could bring myself to travel by rail after that,' she finished. 'I know it's foolish, but if I ever see another train crash I shall turn and run. I couldn't bear it!'

'Nonsense!' His tone was sharp, and her eyes widened. 'You are a nurse, a healer. If such an event happens near you, naturally you must help. It will be automatic,' he insisted.

'I expect you're right,' she agreed for the sake of peace and quiet. She knew she would not be able to help, but there was no point in further discussion. Rail crashes, serious ones, were few and far between, thank God.

The conversation passed to the coronary bypass operation, which was becoming more popular. 'You're aware of the principles, of course? The coronary arteries are bypassed by sections of saphenous vein taken from the patient's own leg.'

'You think that the op is sometimes performed when it isn't strictly necessary?'

'Sometimes, yes. It has become a fashionable operation, rather like tonsils and adenoids were once,' he smiled. 'And, of course, the operation works—we cannot argue with that. But if my team can provide conservative treatment that also works, surely it will be better for the patients? Stress is a great killer and we must do more research, find better ways to tackle it. In this project we're trying various ways of minimising stress. If a patient has the opportunity to talk out his problems to a sympathetic ear then his anxiety is visibly lessened. It is likely his attacks of angina will become less frequent. He has to learn to live with his heart condition, not fight it and cause himself more pain. It is a vicious circle,' he emphasised.

'Not everyone can be spared an operation, though —you mentioned that in the article.' Julia was getting enthusiastic now, and longed to find a way she could help him.

He agreed that not everyone could benefit from the scheme. 'We aren't pioneers,' he stressed, as he sipped a liqueur later. She refused one, finding one glass of wine as much as she could cope with. 'Research is ongoing in various parts of the country, also in the States. It's still new, though, so every project has to be carefully monitored. All the time new treatments are being devised. Research has been carried out elsewhere on the effects of a drug which can be injected into the coronary arteries. If this is done almost immediately after the person has suffered a heart attack, the blood clot that was blocking the artery can be dissolved.'

He surveyed her thoughtfully for a moment, then, to her astonishment, went on to suggest that one of her students might like to work on his ward. 'If you still wish me to take one?' he added.

'Yes, please! Can you find room for one now?' This was unexpectedly good news. She had a suitable student lined up, but because he was so adamant about it, she had decided to leave the subject for a while. She couldn't help wondering why he had changed his mind so abruptly. It was agreed that a third-year would be warded on Tudor the following week. It would be part of the girl's medical module and the experience gained would be invaluable.

Paul Konrad finished his drink, and, glancing at the clock, Julia was amazed to find that it was after ten. So much time had passed and she hadn't begun to get to the bottom of the enigma. 'Which part of Europe do you come from?' she asked boldly, afraid that she would not get another opportunity. He was hardly likely to invite her out again.

He leaned closer, and her lips parted of their own volition. It was all she could do to keep her eyelids from closing. That was an automatic reflex when a handsome animal like Paul Konrad approached!

'You aren't really interested in my past, are you?' His voice was low, throaty.

'Yes, I am!' she protested. 'You intrigue me.' Honesty was the best policy.

'Do I? In what way, Sister Carr?'

'Please stop calling me Sister Carr! We're not on duty now. You make me feel like a . . . a nanny!' she said sternly. 'My name is Julia, off duty.'

'Well, Julia off duty, shall we go?' His teasing tone brought a reluctant smile to her mouth. In the nicest possible way she had been told to mind her own business, but she could not resent it. What business was it of anyone where he came from or what his parents did or what his previous nationality had been? It surely wasn't *her* business, she told herself firmly.

She was nervous as they began on the short drive home. Ought she to invite him in for coffee? He'd already had two cups at the restaurant so wouldn't want any more. Better not to ask him in. He might think she was throwing herself at him, like Linda Greene. She had no fear now that he intended raining passionate kisses on her unyielding mouth or that he had wandering hands. His manner during dinner suggested only that he wanted to talk about his project and, more importantly, that he enjoyed dining out and appreciated a woman's company.

'I like that dress.' He broke the silence as they neared her flat.

'Do you? I've had it years!' she laughed, pleased that he'd even noticed what she wore. Her remark about flowery compliments must have struck oil and that was why he hadn't commented on her appearance this evening. You can't have it both ways, Julia, she remonstrated with herself as the big car drew up outside the house. Either you want his compliments or you don't. And you do—you know you do.

He got out to release the catch for her, although she was perfectly capable of doing so for herself. It was pleasant to be treated like a woman again, like a precious possession. It had been so long . . .

Her eyes darkened with a sadness she could not

express in words, as he accompanied her to the front door. Now, Julia, now! Invite him in, live dangerously! her heart commanded. So, with a warm smile, she invited him up for coffee.

Light came from the lantern at the front door. It illuminated the scene yet threw the consultant's face into shadow, so she couldn't read his expression as he politely declined. 'Tomorrow is another working day for us both, Julia.' His voice was the merest caress, and her name sounded beautiful. 'Good night, sleep well,' he said softly.

'Good nigh——' she began, then his mouth descended on hers and, from far away, she heard sweet music. Her arms crept around his neck and she pressed herself against him, seeking sanctuary in his arms.

'Thank you for a beautiful evening, my Julia,' he murmured against her hair. Then, before she could recover her composure, he left her.

Like an automaton, she put her key in the lock, then closed the front door, leaning against it for a moment as she struggled to regain her composure. The other flats were all occupied and her pride wouldn't let her be seen in such a state of emotional disarray.

She almost ran up the stairs, not stopping till she reached the flat. She switched on all the lights briefly, as was her habit when returning after dark. Then she switched off the sitting-room light before going over to close the faded curtains. His car was still there; evidently he was watching to see that she got upstairs safely. Her lips curved into a tremulous smile. That he should care, should take the trouble to wait, was wonderful. And unusual in a man, in her sad experience. It was a sash window and she raised the bottom half, and waved. In response the interior light of the car was flicked on and then off again, and the car pulled out, her eyes following it until she could no longer see its tail-lights.

Swiftly she drew the curtains, then put a hand wonderingly to her face. He had called her 'my Julia'!

CHAPTER FOUR

IT wasn't until the next morning that Julia realised she still had the magazine containing Paul's article. Although he hadn't suggested she call him by his first name, after last night she couldn't think of him as 'Dr P. Konrad, Consultant in cardiac medicine'. He would be 'Paul' in her innermost thoughts. She only hoped she wasn't falling for the man—that would be a tragedy. Despite the fact that he had not made the expected pass, he had kissed her, and she couldn't deny that the touch of his lips on hers did strange, inexplicable things to her heartbeat.

Still, it meant nothing to either of them. What was a kiss, anyway?

By the time she was ready to go on duty she had convinced herself that his kiss meant as little to her as it did to him. Nevertheless, she smiled tenderly to herself as she smoothed out the article for yet one more read. Gently she ran her fingers over the page, trying to conjure up a portrait of Paul, trying to breathe life into yesterday's memory, but she could not. She stared down at the cold, lifeless page, then shrugged philosophically. She was behaving like a lovesick young girl. Stop it, Julia! she admonished herself. Briefly she re-read the points she found most interesting: that rehabilitation for a normal life was the prime goal. As well as medical and nursing staff, the team should consist of occupational therapists and physiotherapists plus lay people who could offer special skills to aid the healing process.

Whatever tasks the patient found most relaxing should be encouraged.

She paused, wondering if *she* had a special skill to offer. Art therapy was mentioned as a possibility, but there wasn't an artist among the women she'd met on Tudor Ward. No, it wasn't practicable. They would want a trained and skilled artist. She was a mere beginner, a dabbler. Watercolour painting and drawing were hobbies she had enjoyed as a child, inheriting her talents from her mother. Although nursing had taken all her spare time later, she had returned to painting when John died, finding it soothing. It had certainly helped her and she felt it could be equally beneficial to heart patients. Those on Tudor Ward were people whose hearts reacted abnormally to stress. They became over-stressed, over-anxious, overtired. Surely art could play a part in their cure?

She hadn't touched her artists' brushes for over a year. With all the extra work she had had with her mother, then being short-staffed at St Crispin's, she simply hadn't found the time to return to her hobby. She hadn't felt the need, either. She was in equilibrium with her surroundings. She didn't need to use art as a therapy any more, but perhaps she could help those who did.

Over the weekend she prepared one or two small sketches to show Paul. Of course, if the patients had no talent for drawing, their inability to participate fully might cause them more stress. She didn't want them to feel that they were failures, but there was no reason why they could not experiment with painting, in watercolour or even oils, for the more ambitious. She knew the Friends of the Hospital would help with the necessary funds, and she had equipment she no longer needed. The idea of a wall mural occurred to her as well. These were commonplace in psychiatric hospitals and in the paediatric section of St Crispin's. Why shouldn't Tudor Ward have one?

She broached the subject hesitantly to Paul, wondering as she did so if she was keen to help his patients for *his* sake rather than theirs. She honestly didn't know the answer, but if she found herself visiting the ward only when he was around, then she would be heartily ashamed of herself.

To her chagrin, he did not appear keen on her idea. Or perhaps the idea was acceptable but for some reason he did not want her on Tudor Ward. They were in her office at the School of Nursing. Dr Konrad had promised the Principal Tutor that he would give a lecture on new forms of cardiac therapy to a group of senior students. Finding him waiting in her office was an unexpected bonus for Julia.

'The idea is an excellent one—in theory,' he said cautiously, standing with his back half to her as he stared out of her window. 'We have many volunteers and professionals offering various types of recreational therapy.'

'Perhaps they have enough "therapies" inflicted on them for the present.' She deliberately kept her tone light, not wanting him to sense her disappointment. And she *was* disappointed. It hung like a big black cloud over her and made her angry, but with herself, not him. She hadn't the right to get upset over such a small matter. He knew what was best for his patients.

Her fingers ached to touch his thick, dark hair, and she had an excellent view of the way it only just cleared his collar. Savagely she bit her lip, horrified at her reaction to his nearness. She had never felt this way about a man before—no, not even about her beloved John, who was good and kind and gentle, with no trace of the leashed ruthlessness which she sensed in this man. She felt the saltiness of blood on her lower lip and hastily licked it away.

'It might be possible.' After what seemed an eternity, he turned his head, watching her from under half-closed eyelids. His lashes were very black against his cheeks, and she wanted to stroke them.

Fighting down the hysterical urge to laugh, she smiled politely, managing to avoid his penetrating gaze by shuffling some papers on her desk. 'It might be a good idea to ask your patients if they would like to do a spot of painting?' she suggested.

'The very sick ones don't want to be asked anything. They simply want to be made well with the minimum effort on their part,' he pointed out blandly. 'Those on the mend might be interested. I'll see what Sister Greene thinks.'

'Yes, of course,' Julia agreed. She had forgotten that Linda Greene co-ordinated the various healers. It wasn't likely that the idea would get off the ground now.

To her surprise, Linda gave a cautious welcome to the idea. 'It might be helpful. After all, Paul is trying out different types of activities for our patients. He's really wonderful,' she enthused, and Julia silently agreed.

'Of course, I haven't any real talent. Perhaps a professional artist would be better,' she felt bound to say.

'Probably. But a professional artist wouldn't have the necessary patience,' Linda pointed out. 'However . . .' She paused dramatically, as Julia waited to hear her fate. This project had suddenly become important to her, and at last she realised that it *was* for the patients' sake. She genuinely wanted to coax them back to health, exactly as she'd done when running a medical ward.

'For some reason,' Linda continued, with a bright smile, 'Paul isn't keen on *you* providing the art therapy.'

'Oh?' Julia kept her own smile firmly in place and tried not to appear too interested in any explanation that might be forthcoming.

Her colleague looked disappointed that Julia had no more comment than that. 'I thought you might be able to throw some light on the matter?' she threw in casually.

Julia shook her head. 'If Dr Konrad doesn't want me on Tudor then there's no more to be said. It's a great pity, though.'

'Yes, it is,' Linda agreed. 'I still believe it's an excellent idea and if we could get some *other* Sister to provide the necessary expertise, I see no reason why it shouldn't go ahead. It's a wonderful idea, and I'll let you know when Paul and I find someone.'

Linda disappeared through the door leading to Tudor, leaving Julia to make her way disconsolately to the School. Paul evidently did not want her on his ward —why, she could not imagine. Now there was to be a student warded there, occasional visits from a clinical teacher would be necessary. Evidently Paul expected her to send one of her subordinates. He was out of luck, because *she* intended supervising the student!

The following day she sent Student Nurse Neville to Tudor Ward. Julia had chosen her to begin the experiment because she would be taking her Finals in October and had finished her normal ward allocation, so any out-of-the-ordinary experience would be helpful. It would be equally helpful to Julia herself, because she needed to be well informed on new procedures, new techniques, different forms of therapy.

Later that morning, she went along to Tudor, both to check on Nurse Neville and to see the patients for

herself. There might be some interesting nursing procedures going on and she found the prospect exciting.
Paul's research project, though small, was infusing new
life into the hospital. She wondered if she dared ask him
to take a second student but decided not to labour the
point. Sister Greene didn't want learners on that ward
because she felt it interfered with the treatments, so
Student Nurse Neville would have to soldier on by
herself for the time being.

Linda Greene was less than pleased to see her, that
much was obvious, and Julia's temper rose. 'If you've
had an argument with someone,' she began, 'please
don't take it out on me, Linda. It wasn't *my* fault.'

Linda sniffed. 'You were the one who suggested
students. Paul wouldn't have thought of it otherwise.'

Julia raised a brow. 'You're generally as keen as I am
on teaching the youngsters. This ward is a valuable
training opportunity for them.'

'Oh, I know, but Tudor is special. There isn't time to
supervise learners. They get in the way and have to
be——'

'One senior third-year is not learners en masse, Linda.
Is Nurse Neville a problem to you? If she is, I'll send
someone else, but since Dr Konrad said I could place
a student here, I intend to do so.' Julia was adamant
on that point. How could the staff nurses of tomorrow learn if they were excluded from projects like
Tudor?

The student herself wasn't a problem, apparently.
The problem was that both the consultant and the Ward
Sister really wanted only trained nurses, preferably
those with experience in nursing cardiac patients.

'I'll see that someone from the school visits Tudor
every weekday,' Julia promised. She could not always

spare the time, but Wendy Hamilton would be keen to come on other occasions.

She found her student enthusiastically participating in relaxation therapy with three of the patients, one of them Mrs Hammond. The woman looked a lot fitter than on the first occasion Julia had met her, though clearly she wasn't yet cured. The patients lay on comfortable mattresses at one end of the ward where the relaxation exercises were supervised by Nell, their occupational therapist. Julia knew that Nell was working full time on Tudor now, helping to get Paul's project off to a good start. Soothing music came from a cassette and she found her own eyes half-closing as she listened.

Once the session was over, she questioned her student about her morning's work. 'It's the usual medical ward routine, Sister. There's bedmaking, medicine rounds, food to be served, that sort of thing.' She indicated Mrs Hammond, who was sitting quietly in a chair now. 'That patient has made a remarkable recovery, according to Dr Konrad. He's really great!' she went on, and Julia hid a smile. Another convert for the dark-eyed doctor! 'Mrs Hammond has learned to cope better with the problems that brought her in here, but he won't discharge her yet. She wants to go home now and she's fretting over it,' the student told her.

Wondering how Paul would deal with the situation, Julia went to speak to Mrs Hammond. 'My student tells me you're getting along well, Mrs Hammond,' she smiled.

'Oh, I am, Sister. I feel remarkably well. I want to get back home, but Doctor won't let me.' She appealed to Julia. 'Can't you persuade him to change his mind?'

'I doubt if anyone can persuade him,' Julia said firmly, and a reluctant smile crossed the patient's face.

'You're probably right, Sister. Yet it's such a waste of time sitting here when I could be getting on with my business. I feel so angry with myself for getting in this state, and now I've lost a week or more out of my life!' she complained.

Before Julia could speak, Nurse Neville plucked at her sleeve. Surprised, she glanced up, to find Paul Konrad glowering at her, out of the patient's sight.

'Losing a week is better than losing the rest of your life, surely?' he said smoothly, as he moved nearer.

'Oh yes, Doctor,' Mrs Hammond said meekly.

Knowing that the consultant somehow resented her presence on the ward, Julia left the patient and went to speak to those in bed or sitting in chairs. She would not allow him to chase her from the ward. She had a duty to Nurse Neville. In any case, she had promised Linda that the student would not be left unsupervised for long periods.

Removing herself from the consultant's disapproving gaze, she helped serve the patients' elevenses. There were eight patients now, with Mrs Hammond remaining the lone woman. Of the eight, she was by far the fittest. Two of the men Julia had seen previously had been discharged, one to his home, the other to the surgical side of the hospital where a coronary bypass operation was to be performed. On Tudor they had built up his strength and put him in a more relaxed frame of mind, so he was thus in better shape to withstand what was, after all, open-heart surgery, with all its attendant risks.

Two of the men, in the cubicles nearest the door, were sleeping peacefully and they would be woken at lunch-time for a light meal or whatever liquids they fancied. 'Sleep is very important,' Chris Neville said firmly, perhaps not realising that Julia had read the consultant's article.

'In Mr Elphick's case,' Nurse Neville indicated the younger of the two men, 'we discourage visitors—at least for the time being. His wife was threatening to leave him. Now she's overcome with remorse, Sister says, and wants to visit, but at the moment he isn't allowed anybody. Dr Konrad says his system needs all the rest it can get. Later on, Mrs Elphick will be encouraged to come and perhaps they'll be able to sort out their problems, with help.'

The student had evidently spent an interesting morning on the ward, and the rest of her conversation was peppered with references to Dr Konrad. He had taken her under his wing, it appeared, so perhaps it was only Linda Greene who did not want learners—maybe because she did not want Julia on the ward.

Julia was shepherding a small group around Brer Rabbit ward when she next met up with Paul Konrad. Brer Rabbit was a ward of six beds and cots reserved for children with heart problems. Dr Konrad was far from her mind as she led her group to the ward's dayroom. The three new students she had brought included Sally Dalton. Having found out by now which students needed the most help and encouragement, she kept a special eye on them. Apart from Sally, another three needed extra guidance, or so she and the other clinical teachers thought, and one of these was off sick already.

Julia had scarcely begun her pep talk when she became aware of Dr Konrad. He moved silently for a big man, and she raised startled eyes to his, convinced for a moment that her imagination had conjured him up.

'I'm here to examine one of the patients, Sister Carr,'

he said formally, his gaze impersonal, his demeanour as autocratic and forbidding as on that first meeting. Hard to believe now that he'd called her 'my Julia'. Perhaps she had dreamt it all. 'No doubt your young ladies would care to watch,' he went on, surprising her, for she had thought he was objecting to their presence on the ward.

'Yes, please, Doctor,' was her swift response, and they trooped out after him. Sally began to edge nearer the consultant, though he took no notice of her at all, and if Julia hadn't known better she would have assumed they were complete strangers. It was odd. Rather sad, too, the way Sally tried to be near him. It had happened before. It was yet one more puzzling dilemma and Julia intended to solve it if she could. Indicating to Sally that she must keep with the other two, she listened to the brief whispered exchange between the Ward Sister and the consultant. The child he was to see, Simon, suffered from a congenital disease of the heart known as Fallot's tetralogy. This was a combination of heart disorders including pulmonary stenosis—narrowing of the pulmonary valve so that it obstructed the blood going to the lungs from the lower right side of the heart. To improve the quality of life for such patients, surgery was necessary, and their heart surgeon, Mr Almazan, had asked for Paul Konrad's opinion on the boy's condition. It was possible he might be moved to Tudor for preparations, though he wasn't part of the research project.

Julia and her students watched as Paul conducted a thorough examination of the cyanosed boy. He lay apathetically, big grey eyes watching the group without interest. The cyanosis, or purplish-blue colouring, was very marked, and Julia's heart ached for him. In these cases it was possible to perform an operation which would allow a more adequate flow of blood into the lungs, and she wondered what decision would be made about Simon. He had undergone extensive tests, but the final decision rested with the doctors and the parents.

They left Simon to the care of his special nurse, and a thoughtful Julia led her group towards the other children. It had surprised her that Paul was so good with the boy, though she ought not to be surprised after the way he had taken care of little Tim Plummer. Yet he appeared too aloof, too remote, to really understand children. She was sure now that he actually *liked* them. Covertly, she watched as he smiled down at a small girl. Karen wasn't expected to live, but nothing in the consultant's manner suggested pity, nor did he speak cheerfully to her, so many empty words as other doctors had done. He perched on the edge of her bed and held her tiny blueish-tinged hand between his big ones, perhaps willing his touch to send confidence through Karen, a lifeline almost, Julia mused. Then Sally was at her elbow with a query, and she turned her attention to the students, wondering as she did so if Paul Konrad had any children.

Later, it was but a short step from that thought to another one—was Sally Dalton his daughter? It wasn't a new thought, but it came back with remarkable force. They were both tall and brown-eyed, and the doctor had a certain way of smiling. His lips curved ever so slightly and the smile that emerged did so slowly and carefully, rather as if he was unused to smiling. Perhaps for him life had been no laughing matter. Sally smiled in much the same way. That was why the girl seemed so familiar—her mannerisms resembled those of Paul Konrad.

Once the idea was in her mind, Julia could not rid herself of it. Their relationship must be why Sally tried to get close to him on the wards, wordlessly seeking reassurance from a much-loved parent. Her mother, according to Wendy, was a cold personality, and perhaps the girl had only Paul to confide in.

Almost without her being aware of it, the doodles she was making on her pad became a face—Sally's face. Perturbed, she tore the page off the pad and screwed it up, intending to drop it into the waste bin, yet she could not. Carefully smoothing out the paper, she forced herself to analyse the face she had drawn. Sally was pretty, with an oval face and big, wide-spaced dark eyes, the blackness of her long lashes startling against her pale skin.

Knowing it was inevitable, she sketched the consultant, a man with similar wide-spaced eyes and silky black eyelashes. The mouth, too, was a larger version of Sally's, the lower lip full and sensual. She compared the two drawings and saw again the remarkable resemblance. Then she heard voices in the corridor and quickly slipped the sketches into her personal drawer, snapping it shut just as the Principal Tutor appeared.

She intended to take the sketches home with her, not wanting anyone to guess the consultant's secret, but by the time she had answered umpteen phone calls and dealt with a number of queries from learners, it was nearly six. In her rush to escape from the confines of the office, she forgot the sketches. They were safe enough, she reasoned. The drawer was locked and it wasn't likely anyone would be in her office before she returned after the weekend.

By Sunday morning she had completed several further drawings of Paul Konrad. They weren't very good, she acknowledged, her drawing being rusty after so long. They did not do him justice, either. His handsomeness was elusive, enigmatic, like the man himself. He had good bone structure and the harsh planes and lines of his face were a challenge to her skill. Yet she felt she had failed. Not believing that practice made perfect, she nonetheless persevered, and was congratulating herself on a passable image, when the doorbell rang. It wasn't the downstairs one, it was her own bell and, surprised, she pushed the pad to one side and carefully covered it over before going to see who was at the door.

When she inched the door open she was astonished to find Sally Dalton hovering outside. 'Do come in, Nurse,' Julia said warmly, managing to hide her surprise. She wasn't altogether pleased to be disturbed while sketching the consultant, but all the learners knew her address, and she was always willing to see them in private if they had some special problem.

She had to repeat her invitation before the girl ventured in. 'I'm sorry to bother you, Sister Carr, but one of the girls said you didn't mind students coming and . . .' Her voice trailed off as Julia led the way to the sitting-room, a hasty glance towards her pad reassuring her that the drawings weren't visible.

They sat companionably in the sitting-room sipping refreshing orange squash while Sally gazed about her with interest. 'That's a local view, isn't it? Uncle Paul took us there for a drive.' She pointed to one of Julia's own paintings, a delicate watercolour depicting Chanctonbury Ring at sunrise.

Pleased that the girl recognised it, Julia nodded. 'It isn't very good, I'm afraid. I can sketch better than I can paint,' she admitted, gazing up thoughtfully at the view. It wasn't a new painting by any means. 'My husband was alive then,' she murmured, without meaning to mention him. The words just slipped out, and Sally's big dark eyes showed her sympathy. Eyes so like . . . Quickly she shut out the thought.

'Well,' she said brightly, 'what is it I can do for you? Are you having trouble with this weekend's project?' The tutor set all the new learners a project each week, and this one was on the heart and lungs. Of all people, this girl ought to get top marks for that.

'Yes,' Sally mumbled, producing her workbook. 'I was getting on with it, but there were bits I didn't understand. Mother said I should ask Uncle—I mean Dr Konrad, but I didn't want to bother him. He isn't well, you know,' she rushed on, and Julia frowned.

'No, I didn't know. I'm sorry. He looked healthy enough when I saw him on Brer Rabbit Ward.'

'He isn't sick exactly, but he's not himself. He's preoccupied and moody. Mother says she's never known him like this,' she went on candidly.

Julia didn't know what to say. She ought not to encourage a mere student to discuss the consultant's moods. 'I really don't think we should discuss Dr Konrad behind his back,' she said finally, and the girl flushed.

'No, of course not, Sister. Mother said I shouldn't talk about him. But I like talking about him!' she protested. 'He's like a father to me,' she went on, each word making Julia feel more uncomfortable and sad.

Deciding that the subject was too painful to them both, she suggested that Sally show her what work she had prepared. Soon they were poring over the workbook, which was fully of neatly-written notes and beautifully-drawn diagrams.

'Did you draw these?' she asked in astonishment, and Sally nodded. 'They're better than my drawings. Much better,' Julia went on.

'I've always liked art, but I'm not up to professional standard, my teacher said,' confided Sally. 'I do portraits as well. Here.' She rifled in her bag and produced a small, slightly creased drawing. 'That's Uncle Paul,' she said, unnecessarily.

Julia caught her breath sharply. It was unmistakably Paul Konrad. Sally had caught that wistful, half-smiling expression that had eluded her earlier. There was a depth of sadness in the deep-set eyes that she found arresting. Certainly the girl had a great deal of talent.

'This one is Lucy.' Sally produced a smaller drawing. 'She was Uncle Paul's wife,' she added.

'Uncle Paul's wife,' Julia said bemusedly. 'She must have been beautiful.' The drawing was of a rather younger woman than she had visualised as the doctor's wife. Long, straight hair framed a round face and heightened the sitter's sweet expression. The eyes were large and luminous and appeared light, as did the hair.

'She died of leukaemia. Uncle Paul was very cut up,' Sally offered, as Julia stared at the picture.

'I'm sorry,' she said quietly, handing the two pictures back. Sorry was an inadequate word in the circumstances, but what else could she say?

She got out her extra-large coloured diagrams of the heart and began her explanation for the student's benefit. 'The heart is a pump, basically, though it's one of the vital organs of the body. It pumps the blood around the body. And as you know,' she went on, 'blood itself is the transport system that carries nutrients, vitamins and so on wherever they're needed. Heart and lungs are intimately connected by the blood vessels, including the aorta.' She pointed to the aorta. 'That is the largest artery. It——' She was interrupted by the bell, and smiled wryly. 'It sounds as if you're not the only student who's having difficulty!'

It wasn't a student, it was the consultant cardiologist, and Julia paused momentarily before inviting him in. 'Were you looking for Nurse Dalton? I'm just explaining the mechanism of blood supply.' She was flustered, her customary cool deserting her with a vengeance.

She wore an old cotton dress and cardigan, her bare feet thrust into a dilapidated pair of slippers. Paul's casual wear of perfectly-fitting cords and checked shirt made her feel sluttish. It was unlike her not to bother. Even when she wasn't expecting anybody, she tried to look neat, at the very least. The consultant *would* have to catch her the one day she hadn't made the effort! She wasn't sure, either, that she cared for Paul to see where she lived. In some ways it was a violation of her privacy, and she felt stripped bare. Here was her life laid out before him.

Sally greeted him by flinging her arms around his neck, and Julia found the scene strangely touching. She wasn't sure now that she'd got her sums right. Seeing the portrait of Lucy it seemed unlikely he would stray in the direction of another woman, but whatever the facts, Sally clearly adored the man. It wasn't the silly crush that young girls sometimes had for a much older man. There was nothing sexual about it, and she obviously regarded him as a substitute father.

When he saw the heart diagrams he smiled, dark eyes surveying Julia. 'Is that the week's work?'

'Yes . . . yes, it is, Doctor. Would you care to offer a little guidance?' Julia asked hesitantly, recalling what Sally said about the consultant being moodier than usual.

He agreed readily, though, and afterwards Sally

helped Julia to put the medical diagrams away. She refused a cup of tea, as did the consultant. 'I'm sure Nurse Dalton has taken up enough of your time already,' he said formally.

'I'm always pleased to see students, Doctor,' she replied, her tone slightly reproving. She didn't want to put the girl off; there might be other occasions when she needed someone to confide in.

'Of course, Sister.' She was sure she detected a hint of mockery in his tone and she was irritated by it. Unwilling to be mocked, she unthinkingly picked up her sketch pad and held it defensively to her breasts.

The gesture must have amused him, for there was a gleam of devilment in his eyes now. 'Did I offend you, Sister?' His voice was low, meant for her ears alone.

Flushing, she glanced across at Sally, who appeared lost in contemplation of the Chanctonbury Ring painting. 'I can't think what you mean, Dr Konrad,' she said clearly, causing the girl to swing round. 'I'll see you out,' she went on, with a sweet smile for Sally's benefit. 'If ever you want to see me—on *any* matter,' she emphasised, 'you know where I am, Nurse.'

Sally nodded. Then she noticed the sketch pad. 'Oh, are those your sketches, Sister? May I see? Have you drawn anything like the Ring?'

Horrified, Julia backed away, the book still clutched firmly. 'I . . . No! No, I haven't sketched recently,' she said hurriedly. 'I'll look out some old sketches of pastoral scenes, Nurse,' she offered, as Sally seemed disappointed at not being shown the contents of the pad. 'If I find any, I'll bring them into School tomorrow.'

Feeling at a distinct disadvantage, Julia showed them out, the pad now tucked under her arm. Fortunately, she hadn't torn out the pages, so she wouldn't suffer the

embarrassment of portraits of Dr Paul Konrad and his
supposed daughter fluttering everywhere.

It could not have been more than half an hour later
when the consultant reappeared. Annoyed at being
caught in her oldest clothes, she had hurriedly showered
and changed after they left. It wasn't likely she would
have another visitor, but she owed it to herself.

She applied a thin layer of make-up and just a touch of
deep pink lipstick. Then, dressed in her usual neat
blouse and full skirt, she began on her 'homework'—a
pile of questions on practical nursing which she was
marking on behalf of their tutor. She was sighing over an
extraordinary answer when the doorbell rang.

When she opened the door, she very nearly shut it
again. Swiftly recovering her poise, she pinned a polite
smile to her mouth as she invited Dr Konrad in.

His heavy brows frowned at her. 'Am I intruding?'

'No, not at all, Doctor,' she assured him.

'Since you have changed and perfumed yourself, I
thought you were expecting someone,' he said blandly.

'I changed for my own benefit. Can I offer you some
tea now? Or a glass of squash?'

To her surprise, he now accepted the tea he had
declined earlier. She made a fresh pot and carefully
arranged her best china on the silver tray. The tray was a
wedding gift and came out only on high days and holidays. She decided that entertaining the cardiologist
could be classified as a high day. Nervously, she carried
the tray through from the kitchen. Despite his obvious
good humour, he made her feel uneasy. There was some
kind of electricity in the air whenever they met and,
although exciting, it was unsettling.

Rising from her favourite armchair, he took the tray
from her, and their fingers touched. Trying to appear as

unconcerned by the accidental contact as he was, Julia knelt by the glass-topped coffee table and poured the tea. She was proud of the fact that her hand didn't shake once, not even when he smiled lazily down at her, his gaze at once caressing and thoughtful.

'I forgot to mention my Registrar when I came for Sally,' he began, and she relaxed. Her heartbeats settled down again. Shop-talk was safe ground.

'Oh?' she murmured politely as she stirred her tea. 'I didn't realise you were having one. Is he someone new?'

'It might be a "she" rather than a "he", Julia,' he pointed out gently.

'Of course. I hope she will forgive me,' she said quietly, wondering what kind of gorgeous creature he was getting as Registrar. Competition to work with him would be intense.

A faint sigh escaped her. It was so long since she had felt young and sought-after. Redheads were always in demand, and if she felt middle-aged and neglected, it was entirely her own fault. She *ought* to get out and about more, encourage her admirers at St Crispin's instead of giving them the brush-off. It would do no harm and would not tarnish John's memory at all. She would never love again, but surely a light flirtation would do no harm?

Absently, she brushed back a strand of red-gold hair as she contemplated the future. Once Paul's Registrar arrived, she would come out of her shell and face the world. It was time she did.

Glancing up, she was about to ask him if he wanted more tea, but all thoughts of tea flew out of her head as she read the expression in his eyes. Whatever the charms of his Registrar, at that moment it was clear that Paul Konrad wanted Sister Julia Carr.

CHAPTER FIVE

SHE murmured a weak protest, but when Paul's arms closed about her, she raised her face eagerly. They kissed hungrily, as if meeting again after a long, enforced parting. Alarm bells rang in Julia's head as his kisses became more persuasive, but she ignored the warning, surrendering herself completely to the exquisite pleasure of being in his arms. She protested again, but this time for a different reason, as his mouth momentarily left hers and began a tantalising descent to her throat, which he nuzzled gently. Their hearts beat in unison, she believed, and she longed for those few magic moments to go on for ever.

Then reason returned, the magic evaporated, and she hastily pulled herself free. What was she thinking of? Appalled at her weakness, she resorted to anger, though she had no right to turn on him. She hadn't put up much resistance and he must have thought she was willing.

'That was unfair!' she snapped, putting her hands up to her burning cheeks. 'You had no right to take advantage of me!' Even as she spoke, she realised how trite the words were. She was the one being unfair.

He rose and gazed at her, dark eyes sombre. 'Did I take advantage of you, Julia?' His voice was a mere caress and she retreated a few steps. In this persuasive, seductive mood she could not cope with him.

'No, you didn't. I'm sorry,' she said bleakly, overcome with shame for the eager, hungry way her body had met the demands of his. Desire was still between them, and it wouldn't take much persuasion for her to surrender completely, give to this doctor from nowhere what she'd given to no other man except John. But she could not abandon her principles even for the pleasure Paul's lovemaking would bring. It would sully her husband's memory and it was wicked of her to even contemplate it.

As if reading her mind, he said gently: 'Your husband is dead, my Julia, but you are alive! You can't turn your back on life. Don't shut yourself away. Love and you will be loved in return.' He gripped her wrists as if to emphasise the point. His thumb caressed the pulse spot on her wrist, sending desire coursing through her.

'Love.' Her voice was weary. 'Is that what you call it? Love and sex are two different animals. I'm not a naïve child, Paul.' She spoke his name tentatively, realising that it was the first time. She repeated his name with a kind of desperation, then pulled herself free, crossing over to the window and gazing down unseeingly at the drive below. She wished heartily that she'd never met Dr Paul Konrad, never succumbed to his ruthless charm. He was right, of course. She could not turn her back on life. She must learn to live again. But I can't!—the words exploded in her mind. I can't—not with *this* man. He will take me over, demand complete surrender, then calmly walk away.

No, that way led to heartbreak. He was cold and calculating and knew exactly what he was doing to her. She was just another conquest, like Mrs Dalton and Sister Greene. Just another scalp hanging from the warrior's belt. She half turned, her face grave.

He was watching her, his eyes half closed, a smile

hovering about his mouth. He was dangerous and she simply did not know how to cope. She had enjoyed flirtations before her marriage, but nothing in her life had equipped her to deal with a man like this. The charming, easygoing womaniser was easily dealt with: one simply said 'No' firmly. Eventually the message would sink in. But this man . . .

He eased the tension by an unexpected change of topic. 'I came to ask about Sally. Does she confide in you?'

The atmosphere lightened as desire left her. She felt cold, bereft, as though she would never feel the sunlight on her face again. Shivering a little, she shook her head. 'No, not really. She . . . I don't think she's altogether happy with nursing.'

'It was her choice,' he pointed out, but she couldn't let that pass.

'It seems to have been her mother's choice. Mother wanted Sally to help you in your work—that's why she's here. She's good, capable and kind, gentle with the patients, but she lacks the enthusiasm that's so important in the early stages. Without that she won't survive geriatrics or a really busy surgical ward.'

He gazed thoughtfully at her. 'She wants to help sick people. Perhaps she could train as an occupational therapist?'

'Yes, that occurred to me. Her artwork is very good, but she'll need more than that. Perhaps she could help out on Tudor Ward on a purely voluntary basis for a time?' Julia suggested. She did so want to help on Tudor herself, but Sally's ability was greater than hers. In any case, Paul didn't want *her* on the ward.

It was agreed that the suggestion should come from Julia. Sally would have to fit in art therapy as and when she could. It wouldn't be easy, but it would help to sort out the girl's future.

'That's settled, then,' she said brightly, one hand pressed against her heart as he moved towards her. Partly to her relief and partly to her annoyance, he did not rain passionate kisses upon her eager mouth, or even touch her. They were within touching distance, but there was no way she could make the first move and, it seemed, Paul wasn't going to.

'You look frightened, my Julia,' he said seductively. 'Do I frighten you?'

'Yes,' she breathed, 'you do sometimes. I . . . Is Sally your daughter?' She was angry with herself for asking such a question. She couldn't imagine how she came to blurt it out, but it was a question to which she needed to know the answer.

He appeared undismayed by her forthrightness. 'Do you think she is?'

She licked her dry lips, unwilling to say. 'I don't know. She likes to be near you, tries to please you, and I just wondered . . .' She let her voice trail off, leaving it up to him to say more if he wished.

'I loved my wife very much,' he said instead, and Julia's heart ached for him. 'Lucy.' He spoke the name softly. 'For her there could be no children. I wanted twelve!' he smiled. 'A big family, full of love and laughter. Something I lacked in my own childhood, Julia.'

She smiled wanly. At last he was opening up, showing her a little of the man behind the enigma. Then the shutters closed again, and his eyes were expressionless as he wished her a brief goodbye.

He let himself out, Julia remaining by the window lost in thought. She pressed her fingers to her lips, reliving his kisses, the ecstasy of those few moments in his arms.

Although she would never love again, she was very much afraid that she wanted to spend the rest of her life with the ruthless Dr Paul Konrad, a man for whom she was no more than a passing fancy.

Julia was late getting to work next morning. The car wouldn't start, so she had to seek help from one of the other tenants. Eventually, by muttering to himself under the bonnet, and finally giving the car a good kick, he was able to get it started for her.

It was well past nine o'clock when she eventually arrived at St Crispin's, and she was due on a consultant's ward round at half-past with a group of students. To cap it all, Sally Dalton's mother was waiting to see her and had been there since eight-thirty, having been told that clinical teachers started early.

Luckily Wendy was available and Julia was able to pass the students on to her. Wendy apologised to her before whisking the group off to attend the ward round. Julia caught the word 'drawer' before she disappeared, and couldn't think what it meant at first. It was only later, when Mrs Dalton left, that it hit her. Her colleague must have been looking in the top drawer and seen the sketches of Dr Konrad and Sally Dalton!

Rowena Dalton wasn't in a very good mood when Julia greeted her. 'I'm sorry you were kept waiting, Mrs Dalton, but I had trouble with the car,' she said pleasantly. Her offer of coffee was brusquely refused and Mrs Dalton came straight to the point.

'My Sally tells me she's giving up her training,' she said peremptorily. 'And that *you* are responsible,' she added, her dark eyes flashing.

'As far as I know, Nurse Dalton is continuing at St Crispin's,' Julia said smoothly. 'She isn't sure about nursing, I believe, but I can hardly be responsible for the girl's feelings,' she pointed out calmly.

'No, I suppose not,' Mrs Dalton agreed. Her narrow lips tightened, and Julia thought how old it made her look. She was a little older than Paul, she judged, probably in her early forties, but lines of discontent from nose to mouth, plus dark shadows still visible under the heavily made-up eyes, made her appear older. The bright sunlight streaming in the window was too harsh, unkindly revealing the too-thin face and body.

Julia wondered if she ought to mention Paul's concern over Sally. 'Dr Konrad did ask me how Sally was getting on,' she said at last.

'Oh?' There was a wealth of suspicion in that one word.

'I told him that I thought she would make a good nurse some day. I'm not sure that's what she wants, though, and I wondered if she might be interested in doing occupational therapy training or something in that line.'

'She wants to be a nurse,' Mrs Dalton said stubbornly. 'A *medical* nurse,' she insisted. 'And I intend to see that she carries on. Who are you to suggest she drops nursing?' She half rose.

'I'm a senior clinical teacher,' Julia reminded her, 'and I naturally want what's best for my learners.'

'And I'm her mother!' Mrs Dalton exploded. 'Naturally *I* want what's best for Sally! So does Paul Konrad! He takes a special interest in her. They're very close,' she added, watching Julia's face.

'Yes, I *had* noticed, Mrs Dalton.' Julia rose, extending her hand to the visitor. She wasn't going to waste any more time with her. It was Sally Dalton's life and career that were at stake, and the girl was eighteen, old enough to think for herself and not be too concerned about what her mother wanted.

Ignoring Julia's outstretched hand, Rowena Dalton almost hissed at her: 'Paul is my very good friend, and when he's Sally's stepfather he'll make sure she continues her training. I'll see you in hell before I let you interfere!' She strode out, clashing the door behind her.

Wearily Julia rubbed her eyes. What a woman! Poor Sally. And poor Paul Konrad, too, if he was to be Rowena Dalton's next husband. Of course they richly deserved each other. Yet that was no consolation, and her heart ached quite unaccountably for some time afterwards.

It was nearly lunchtime before she saw Wendy again, and then there was time for only a brief word about work. They met again during the tea-break. She simply had to find out what Wendy meant. The question of the sketches was preying on her mind. The sketches were still in the drawer when she looked, but now they were safely in her bag. No one else must see them. Unfortunately, someone had already seen them, apart from Wendy.

'That's what I was apologising for,' said Wendy as they shared a pot of tea. 'I unlocked your top drawer thinking the exam list was there, and what did I find! A wonderful likeness of our Dr Konrad!' she laughed.

Julia didn't find it funny. 'I wanted to sketch him. He has an interesting face,' she hurried on. 'Not exactly handsome, but——'

'Oh, he is, Julia! How can you say he isn't handsome?' her friend rebuked her. 'Anyway, I saw the other drawing and I couldn't think who it was at first, but Miss Smith said——'

'Miss Smith?' Julia echoed, dread settling on her like a

heavy cloak. 'You showed *my* drawings to the Principal Tutor?'

Wendy shifted uncomfortably. 'Well—yes, I'm afraid I did. At least, she saw them. I didn't go rushing round to her office and thrust them under her nose! She came in behind me and I showed them to her.' Her voice trailed off while Julia sat, stunned.

'What did Miss Smith say?' she asked, striving to keep her voice casual.

'She said how much alike they looked, almost as if they were close relations. Oh, Julia, he isn't Sally Dalton's father, is he? How awful!'

'Of course he isn't!' Julia snapped. 'Don't be silly!'

'I'm not being silly,' Wendy said stubbornly. '*You* sketched them both. Surely you must have seen the resemblance?'

'I like sketching people. I did one of you once—last year, wasn't it?' Julia pointed out. 'It wasn't because you reminded me of anyone in particular. Now, about the exams,' she went on briskly, neatly sidestepping Wendy's further questions. She only hoped the matter would blow over quickly and that Miss Smith wouldn't mention it to anyone. It was hardly likely. She wouldn't want a scandal in the hospital, even a minor one. Paul's secret was safe enough with her. Wendy wasn't a gossip, either. She had an unpleasant feeling in the pit of her stomach, though. If word somehow got back to Paul he would know who to blame.

She was teaching injection techniques when next she saw Paul Konrad. She had five girls from the new set with her, including Sally. Sally's trial on Tudor was to being at the weekend. She would drop in casually and talk to the patients, find out how many were interested in art. Julia had suggested that Sally might try to sketch those of the Tudor patients who were well enough. That would be a promising beginning. After much hesitation, the rather shy girl agreed, then asked Julia if *she* would come to Tudor with her on the Saturday.

Somewhat surprised, Julia agreed. She knew she ought to seek Paul's permission first, but didn't like to mention Sally again. She had, after all, accused him of fathering an illegitimate child. It was hardly an auspicious beginning to a professional relationship!

'You won't be expected to give injections for a few weeks yet, so don't worry,' she explained to the group. They were clustered around the bed of Miss Bennett, a patient on Stuart Ward who needed an intramuscular injection. She was a nervous, tense lady and had refused to allow learners near her until Julia assured her that they wouldn't be giving the injection. She herself would give it, explaining the technique to the students as she did so.

The salient points had been explained in the practical room, and the girls had given injections of sterile water to a series of oranges. This fruit was supposed to be a reasonable approximation to the human skin and tissues, and they could hardly practise on real patients. Julia knew from her own experience how hard it was to give the first real injection. Yet they must try sooner or later. The more skilled injections they watched, the better.

'Nurse Dodd, can you tell us what we have to do before the injection?' The syringe was already filled and she had already gone into the whys and wherefores of drawing up drugs in the ward's clinic.

The student hesitated. 'Oh, yes! You draw a cross on the patient's behind, please, Sister.'

Julia nodded. 'Yes, on the buttocks. Why do we need

to do that, Nurse Dalton?' She smiled encouragingly at Sally.

'It's because of the sciatic nerve, Sister. If you mark a cross on the buttocks with a finger, then inject into the outer, upper quarter, you can be reasonably sure that you won't hit the nerve.'

'Reasonably sure?' echoed Miss Bennett, in dismay. 'Isn't it to make *absolutely* sure?'

'In your case we *are* sure,' Julia said firmly, 'but some people are peculiar, and their sciatic nerve runs a bit awry.'

She gave the injection, after telling the patient what she was about to do. Sally, in particular, appeared fascinated as Julia plunged the needle in, withdrawing the plunger a fraction to make sure she hadn't hit a blood vessel, then injected the drug. She then swabbed the site with a mediswab. 'Always tell the patient, an adult patient, anyway, what you're going to do. It's the patient's body and she has a right to know,' she explained. 'Now what must I do?' After settling Miss Bennett comfortably, she held up the syringe and needle.

'Break the needle off at the hilt so it can't be used again,' Sally put in before anyone else could answer.

'And why do we——' Julia began, then stopped in confusion as Paul Konrad's head appeared through the curtains drawn around the bed.

'When you have time, Sister Carr, I would like a word,' he said coldly, and she nodded, her mind numb. Somehow he'd found out about the sketches and was going to wipe the floor with her!

His head withdrew, and one glance from her quelled the whispering from the students. Quickly she carried on with the lecture, the patient listening as intently as the students. Afterwards, the group went back to school and she went in search of Dr Konrad, her heart cold within her breast.

She found him in the consultants' common-room, and fortunately he was alone. Guilt heightened her colour as she faced him. She tilted her chin a little higher, prepared for his anger.

'I'm giving a reception for my new Registrar, Dr Morland,' he began, catching her off balance. True, he clearly wasn't in a very good mood, but perhaps it had nothing to do with the sketches, after all. 'It's tomorrow, about five-thirty or so. People can drift in when ward duties permit.' His eyes met hers and she was shaken by the chilliness of his gaze. 'I know you are anxious to meet my Registrar.'

'Naturally I'd like to meet her,' she answered. 'Does she know about Sally Dalton? I mean, about the art therapy. It's on Saturday morning,' she rushed on, worried in case he misunderstood her. 'She's going to meet the patients and sound them out,' she went on, since he seemed to be expecting more explanation.

He surveyed her from half-closed eyes, and she was struck anew by his charisma. 'That will be satisfactory, Sister,' he said at last.

'Well then, I'll be getting back,' she said with relief. 'Unless there's anything else?'

'Yes, just one more point, Sister.'

Tense, she waited, knowing that she had no justification for what she had suggested about him and Sally. If only she hadn't sketched them both! He would wonder why she had sketched him, come to think of it. She hoped he wouldn't think it was because she actually *cared* for him. Nothing could be further from the truth.

A malicious expression crossed his face, and Julia had

the insane urge to take to her heels and run. He was actually enjoying this cat-and-mouse game!

'On Friday I'm conducting a major ward round on Tudor. Perhaps you would like to bring a senior group of students and join the round?' That smile appeared then and she wanted to hit him.

She'd been all worked up for nothing! 'Thank you, Doctor. That's most kind of you,' she managed. She struggled hard not to show resentment, but her expressive blue eyes gave her away.

'The reception will be held here, Sister Carr.'

'What? Oh, yes. For Dr Morland,' she murmured, recalling herself to the present with difficulty. 'Is she staying long? I mean, when you return to the States will she stay at St Crispin's?'

He shrugged, the immaculate dark jacket straining against his broad shoulders. 'That all depends. We must wait and see—hm?' His gaze was too penetrating, and she wondered if he read minds as a sideline. Certainly hers wasn't difficult to read at that moment. Dr Morland might stay or she might return home with him. As his wife?

Courteously, he held open the door for her, apparently satisfied that he had torn her nerves to shreds. At the door, he cast a quick glance out into the corridor, then leaned towards her.

Convinced he meant to kiss her and equally convinced that she should slap his smug face, Julia waited. Her lips parted and she half closed her eyes as his face moved nearer. It was a purely instinctive gesture, but he would take it as encouragement and probably despise her for it. Another broken heart to notch up on his wall. Just as their lips were about to meet, there were footsteps and muted voices in the corridor, and they broke apart.

'We will have to find a more private place, Sister,' he chuckled huskily, and her face burned. Frustrated and very, very angry, she hurried away, passing two doctors with barely a glance. She was afraid desire and longing must show in her eyes.

She hated the man! But oh, how she longed to be in his arms! To be literally swept off her sensible feet in their sensible black duty shoes; to be gathered up in his muscular arms and kissed and caressed passionately. And then . . . She nearly sobbed aloud. She was convinced now that he hadn't meant to kiss her, after all. He was still toying with her, wanting her to suffer because of her remarks about him and Sally. He was despicable as well as ruthless. And untrustworthy. And arrogant and spiteful, too. Feeling better after her silent condemnation of the man, Julia walked briskly back to her office. Tomorrow she would meet yet another woman in his life—the mysterious Dr Morland.

It was Wendy who dropped the bombshell, right at Julia's feet. 'But he isn't a "she", Julia!' she exclaimed later, when Julia wondered aloud whether Dr Morland would be beautiful.

'Are you telling me that Dr Morland is *male*?' she demanded, pale with anger.

Wendy nodded. 'Surely Dr Konrad told you? I suppose the question of sex didn't arise?'

Hastily, Julia put in: 'I thought he said Dr Morland was female, but I must have misunderstood him.' She knew quite well that there was no misunderstanding. He had led her on deliberately and hadn't corrected her when she kept referring to the Registrar as 'she'. Another game for the big cat: watch the mouse squirm in agony before delivering the death blow. Just wait till she got her hands on him!

She attended the reception to welcome Dr Morland
—Dr Rob Morland, she now learned. It was held in the
consultants' common-room, and only a choice few were
invited. Julia supposed she ought to feel flattered, but
she knew the real reason for the invitation: Paul Konrad
wanted to humiliate her. He would introduce Dr Morland and then stand back and watch her astonishment
and embarrassment. Typical of the man! Then her in-
nate sense of fairness surfaced and she knew she was
doing him an injustice. He didn't really want to humiliate her. She struggled to find some plausible reason for
his deception but could not. In the end she put it down to
a foreign sense of humour. A lot of his behaviour could
be explained away like that.

So, having given Paul the benefit of the doubt, she
greeted him with a smile as she entered the common-
room. She was one of the first to arrive, and the new man
didn't appear to be there. Paul's dark eyes warmed as he
returned her greeting, and she almost cried aloud in her
despair. Why did he have to be so desirable? Why did he
have to be heavily engaged with umpteen other women,
come to that?

'I hear that Dr Morland is a man, Dr Konrad,' she said
evenly.

He began to smile, then changed his mind as she
watched. 'But yes! Did you think I would have a female
Registrar?'

Julia's lips twitched as she, too, suppressed a smile.
'Yes, I did. I can't imagine what put the idea in my mind,
Doctor.'

'Nor can I. It's very strange,' he mused. Then he
laughed.

It was the first time she'd seen him laugh, really laugh.
Usually it was just that sad, wistful smile. She joined in,

unable to help herself. They could be friends, after all.

Then a very tall young man appeared, his corn-gold hair conspicuous among the dark or grey-haired men present. 'You must meet our charming Sister Carr,' Paul insisted. As he performed the introductions, Julia sized up the newcomer. Dr Morland was taller even than the consultant, though not handsome. His long, lean face would one day be full of humour lines as he was extremely cheerful. He beamed at Julia as he vigorously pumped her hand.

Extricating her hand from his painful grip proved harder than she expected, and her eyes narrowed in suspicion as she wondered whether he, too, collected the scalps of redheads.

'Sorry. Did I break your fingers?' He smiled apologetically as he released her. 'It's the story of my life,' he went on ruefully, running his fingers through his tousled golden hair.

'I don't think you've fractured anything, Dr Morland,' she assured him.

When Dr Morland smiled down at her, she found herself responding. True, her heartbeat didn't quicken, but it was as if the sun had risen in the middle of a stormy night, and she was grateful for its warmth. Then the storm approached, face like thunder and brown eyes shooting celestial lightning at her. Dr Paul Konrad had lost his sunny mood, perhaps believing the Registrar was monopolising her.

'Perhaps you could spare me a moment, Dr Morland.' His voice was bleak, and Julia wondered at it.

'Yes, of course, sir. Naturally.' With a warm smile for Julia the Registrar drifted away and was soon deep in conversation with the senior physiotherapist. The cardiologist, having dragged Dr Morland away, now seemed to have lost interest, and as Julia saw him exchange intimate smiles with Linda Greene, her heart twisted.

Someone thrust a sherry into her hand, and she stared down thoughtfully into its golden depths. She moved around the small gathering, exchanging a word here, a smile there. She saw the new doctor only from across the room. He had a pleasant, easygoing nature and was going to be immensely popular. He would cheer the cardiac patients up. Julia looked forward to meeting him again.

She felt a hand on her arm and swung round, hoping it was the enigmatic Dr Konrad. Linda Greene smiled at her instead, and Julia tried to appear pleased. 'Not a very exciting reception, is it?' remarked Linda. 'Still, it was useful meeting Dr Morland. Seems pleasant enough.'

'Yes, he's remarkably cheerful,' Julia agreed. 'He'll be good for your patients.'

'Mm, I hope so.' Linda sipped her Martini, eyeing Julia covertly. 'He isn't a patch on Paul, though.'

'He's only just arrived, Linda!'

'I didn't mean his medical expertise, my dear.'

'Oh?' Julia kept her voice expressionless, and this seemed to annoy her colleague.

'He hasn't Paul's charisma, his sensuousness—I think that's the right word. Well,' she went on, draining her glass, 'I must get home to change. I'm being taken out to dinner,' she confided, lowering her voice. 'He's taking me to some cosy out-of-town place.'

'I hope you have an enjoyable evening, Linda,' Julia said, proud of her calmness as she watched Linda hurry away. Some cosy out-of-town place. Not the Harlequin where he'd taken her. He couldn't be seen dining with a married woman. Poor Linda, having to be wined and dined in some restaurant in the back of beyond. Lucky Linda, to be enjoying the consultant's company, no matter where they ended up.

Saddened, she had a sudden urge to escape. She didn't want to spend any more time here, dreaming wistfully of what might have been.

CHAPTER SIX

JULIA arrived early for Friday's ward conference on Tudor. What the consultant had to say would be too advanced for Sally Dalton's set, so she took six third-years with her. They were from the same set as Chris Neville, so would obtain the maximum advantage from Dr Konrad's lecture.

Although Paul wasn't there at first, Rob Morland was, and he greeted Julia like an old friend. He was so anxious to be friendly that she warmed to him, but when he paid her a flowery compliment, telling her that he had never seen such beautiful hair, her smile froze.

He looked discomfited. 'Sorry. Did I step on someone's toes?'

Her eyes were cool. 'I beg your pardon, Doctor?'

'It's Rob when we're off duty,' he whispered, 'and I said did I step on someone's toes? Does some lucky guy have the sole right to praise you?'

Julia forgave him. It wasn't fair to punish him just because he wasn't Dr Paul Konrad. 'I don't know any lucky guys,' she whispered back, then hastened to quieten down her students as Paul Konrad strode into the dayroom. Sister Greene wasn't far behind, with another nurse wheeling in the trolley full of case notes. Paul's brows knitted together in a frown when he saw his Registrar standing close to Julia, but Rob stood his ground, much to her surprise. Clearly he wasn't a man to be bullied.

There was a dejected set to Paul's shoulders and Julia

wanted to fling her arms about his neck, draw his weary head down on to her breasts and kiss away his sorrows. To emphasise that she wanted no part of the Registrar's interest, she settled herself on a chair on the other side of her group of nurses, leaving Rob Morland stranded.

'Perhaps you would care to join me, Dr Morland?' Paul suggested, in a chilly tone, and the tall doctor loped across to him, warm smile at the ready.

She surveyed them both from under her golden lashes —two men, two doctors, but so different. The consultant's face might have been hewn out of granite, so expressionless was it. His dark eyes swept over the gathering, and his expression was bleak. In a dark formal suit for a change, and white shirt he was every inch the successful, sought-after consultant. In contrast, his blond subordinate beamed at everyone, his grey eyes alive with good humour. Under the long white coat he certainly wasn't wearing a formal suit, for Julia caught a glimpse of rather baggy yellow cords.

More junior doctors drifted in, then Sister Greene closed the door firmly. The consultant waited until everyone was seated before he began, but betrayed no sign of impatience. Julia made sure that all her group had their notebooks and pens ready. She, too, intended taking notes.

'We have nine patients at present,' Paul Konrad began, his eyes on Julia. 'We're hoping to always keep one bed spare, but . . . the best laid plans often don't work out.'

She shifted uncomfortably. Of course he wasn't actually looking at her, it merely seemed that way. Indeed, his glance fell on others in the group as the discussion proceeded. Yet always those haunting dark eyes found their way back to Julia and she became totally absorbed in what he was saying. No one else mattered. Indeed, she felt that she and Paul were alone, that his words were directed solely at her. It was an eerie feeling and she wondered at the emotion which could cause it. It wasn't love, yet was more than mere attraction. They belonged together.

Hastily she gathered her wits. Her coming was a sheer waste of time if she sat and daydreamed of what might have been.

'Mr Baxter,' he was saying, and she endeavoured to concentrate, scribbling the name in her notebook. He must be new. 'He's aged fifty-two and was admitted yesterday,' the consultant went on. 'He suffers severe bouts of angina, and the attacks are usually brought on when he has an argument at work. I imagine this is a frequent occurrence. Now,' he paused, his gaze falling upon Julia again, 'Sister Carr, does this patient sound a suitable candidate for our therapy? Do you believe we can relieve his stress? Or would you suggest that he will eventually need the bypass operation?'

All her students turned round, eyes expectantly on her. 'What about his coronary arteries, Doctor? Has any narrowing occurred?' she asked. That, surely, was the important point.

The cardiologist shook his head. 'No, there has been no physical narrowing.'

'Then the therapy your team is offering should be sufficient without an operation—plus rest, of course,' she added confidently. It seemed clear-cut to her.

Dr Konrad folded his arms, leaning back against the desk on which the other case notes lay. A wolfish smile crossed his face, and she wondered if he had set a trap for her and she had fallen into it.

'What if he will not rest?'

'Rest is essential,' she said firmly. 'He must be encouraged. He needs a chance to talk over his problems. Once his mind is easy, he should find it easier to sleep, even without drugs or tranquillisers.'

'He is resisting our efforts, Sister,' he said complacently. 'He cannot face up to his problems.'

She wondered if he was deliberately indicating difficulties that did not, in fact, exist. Perhaps it was a test for the students, who were keenly interested in the drama being played out in front of them. 'If he doesn't want to be helped why is he here? I'm sure your team has enough to do without patients like that.'

'He needs our help more than most.' His tone was reproachful, and Julia flushed. Of course he was right, but surely he could have chosen a less public way to put her in her place? Resentment flared for an instant, then died. Mr Baxter was a challenge, and her eyes gleamed.

'Mr Baxter will be a challenge to you all, Dr Konrad,' she said clearly. 'It's a test of your team's ability.'

The consultant nodded approvingly. 'Excellent! You have forestalled me. That was the point I was about to make.'

Pleased that she had done something right in the man's eyes, she felt other eyes upon her. Linda Greene's glance was unfriendly and rather resentful, Julia thought. Then she shrugged. The patients and the learners were more important than petty jealousies. Linda need not think *she* had designs on Paul Konrad!

They began to drift in twos and threes towards the main ward. The dayroom was normally shared between Stuart and Tudor Wards but had been closed off for the duration of the lecture.

Tudor was light and airy and more spacious than the average medical ward. They began with the two female patients, Mrs Hammond, whom Julia had already met, and a newcomer, Mrs McFarland. Of course they couldn't all congregate round each bed. Even if these people were not heart patients, that would have been too much of a good thing. Julia saw to it that her students were dispersed throughout the ward. She herself sat by Mrs McFarland while the doctors discussed Mrs Hammond's condition with her.

She knew from the discussion that Mrs McFarland was considered suitable for the bypass operation, though all steps were being taken to avoid it. In any case, she would need a period of preparation first. Her strength needed building up and she had to learn to relax more—something that these patients found wellnigh impossible. They lived on their nerves. Julia held a whispered conversation with the patient before the team gravitated towards them.

The beds were widely spaced, much more so than was usual in a ward, so some degree of privacy was afforded. Julia patted the woman's hand comfortingly, as the patient poured out her worries. She was in her sixties and the strain of bringing up a large family was telling on her at last. She confided that her eldest son was in prison for embezzlement and that was her greatest worry. 'He's been such a good boy to me, Sister,' she went on. 'This was his first mistake, I'm sure of it, but the police said it's been going on for some time.'

Then Dr Konrad appeared and Mrs McFarland immediately perked up. Letting go of Julia's hand, she grasped his instead, beaming up at him. It seemed to Julia that strength flowed from the doctor to his patient. If sheer willpower and determination and, yes, a trace of ruthlessness, could help to cure her then Dr Konrad was the man to provide it.

He smiled seductively at the patient, who went quite pink with pleasure. Of course Julia had risen when he approached that side of the cubicle, but he indicated that she should stay where she was. He settled himself on the edge of the bed, something strictly forbidden, and began to talk easily to the woman. Julia beckoned one of her students over to hear what the consultant had to say.

To her surprise, he spoke only in general terms, not touching on her personal worries. They discussed the fine weather, what Mrs McFarland had been doing that morning in the way of therapy. He also mentioned that although he had little time, he had an enormous garden he was trying to tame and that he enjoyed watching things grow.

Mrs McFarland nodded emphatically. 'So do I, Doctor. So do I. Not that I've ever had the patience to do much gardening. It was my mother who had green fingers—she used to talk to the plants!' She giggled girlishly, and Julia could see Paul's mind working. She had no doubt that pot-plants would mysteriously appear on Tudor in future!

Ted Baxter, by contrast, was a thin, miserable man with a long face and very little hair. He seemed a lot older than fifty-two, Julia considered, and his face was heavily lined. He still bore the faint scent of tobacco and when he opened his mouth she could see his stained, irregular teeth. He had little to say to any of them, confining his remarks to essential monosyllables as the Registrar examined him under the watchful eye of Paul Konrad.

Julia smiled but got no response. When she placed her cool hand over his, he jerked away as if disliking physical contact. From what Paul said in the dayroom, she knew that Mr Baxter was a widower and had been for many years. He lived alone in a Council flat in a poor area of the town and was employed as a porter in a local factory. Soon the factory was to close and he would be redundant. With his health record it was unlikely he would get another job—another worry for his overtaxed heart to cope with. He was altogether an unattractive man, yet she could understand what Paul meant: Mr Baxter needed to be here.

The archetypal patient was, of course, the well-fed businessman who both drank and smoked to excess. A man with pressing business worries or a demanding job and a lifestyle which included much lavish entertaining, big lunches, cocktail parties and the like. Julia knew the unit had only one such person. Most people like that had private health insurance and would not come into a National Health hospital except in emergency. What was often forgotten was that poorer people also had business worries—the single-handed electrician or plumber, for example. Having seen Tudor Ward, she was only now beginning to realise how many of these people there were. Often those in lower income brackets had more cause for frustration. They saw all the goodies on display but could only watch while others enjoyed them. Wants created needs, and so the vicious spiral continued. Ted Baxter had precious little in life, it seemed to her, and she was determined to see what she could do for him. It was a challenge, and she had never backed off from a challenge yet.

They spent less time with the others, most of whom would get up once the round was over. Occupational therapy awaited them, plus various other activities.

Glancing round for the consultant, she saw him walking away from the last bed, Linda Greene hanging on his every word. As Julia watched, unable to tear her eyes away, Paul laughed down at Sister Greene and she put her hand possessively on his arm and gazed up at him in frank admiration.

Sad-eyed, Julia gathered her brood together and sent them off to the school, warning them that she wanted an essay written on the morning's round. Adjusting her lace cap, which had become loosened, she made for the door. She had been about to thank Paul for his kindness, but he was too busy to notice her leave. She would drop him a courteous note later. Courtesy cost nothing, and it was kind of him to let the students attend his round.

'Sister—wait! You must have even longer legs than I thought.' Rob Morland grinned down at her, his gaze shrewd.

He knows how I feel about Paul, she mused. Does it show in my face, I wonder?

'How about taking pity on a newcomer and joining him for a coffee tomorrow morning?' he suggested, matching his steps with hers as they headed towards the consultants' common-room. Julia hadn't intended going that way, but it didn't seem to matter.

'Saturday? I'd like—Oh, I can't! I'm really sorry, Dr . . . Rob,' she murmured, then explained about the art therapy and the junior student she was bringing to Tudor Ward.

'That's okay by me. Bring her along,' Rob said casually. 'Better still, I'll take you both to lunch,' he offered, and she was touched by his generosity.

She wasn't sure she should accept for Sally. After all, Mrs Dalton might have other plans for her daughter. But for herself she had no doubts. 'That's very sweet of you. I'd like to have lunch with you tomorrow.' She smiled at him just as Paul Konrad passed. He nodded to them both but didn't stop, and she wondered if he had overheard her accepting the Registrar's invitation.

Why shouldn't she dine with Dr Morland? He was very personable. He might be good for her. It was time she had someone to cheer her up, bring her out of her homemade shell. Never mind Paul Konrad.

Forget Paul Konrad, she told herself, wondering as she did so if it would ever be possible to forget such a man.

Next morning was very warm, with just the faintest of breezes. A perfect day for a stroll on the South Downs, yet duty called. Julia had promised Sally Dalton that she would ease her gently into Tudor Ward and introduce her to the staff, at least. Sister Greene would not be on duty until Sunday afternoon, and that was a good thing, Julia decided. She didn't want to listen to details of her evening out with Paul Konrad. The woman was married, after all, and it wouldn't do Paul's career any good. As he was only visiting it didn't matter so much, perhaps, but the resultant gossip would cause him to lose face in front of his junior doctors. For a man like him, loss of face was a serious matter.

Of course, Julia acknowledged as she set out for the hospital, Paul Konrad, his career and his private life were no concern of hers. She mustn't interfere. Paul was perfectly capable of taking care of himself. Her eyes darkened with an overwhelming sadness. Paul didn't need her; he didn't need anyone. How she wished he did! Despite her determination to continue alone, he was becoming more and more important to her. She wasn't sure why. Maybe it was jealousy. She frowned. Jealousy of whom? Mrs Dalton? Sister Greene? Hardly. She had no doubt that he treated them both in a cavalier fashion. They would have to fit in with *his* schedule, go

Dear Susan,

Your special introductory offer of 4 free books is too good to miss. I understand they are mine to keep together with the free Tote Bag.

Please also reserve a Mills & Boon Temptation subscription for me. If I decide to subscribe, I shall receive six new books every two months for £7.20* post and packing free. If I decide not to subscribe I shall write and tell you within 10 days. The free books and Tote Bag will be mine to keep in either case.

I understand that I may cancel or suspend my subscription at any time simply by writing to you. I am over 18 years of age.

Signature _____

Name _____

Address _____

_____

Postcode _____   8A6TEA

*Same price as the books in the shops.

YOURS FREE!

Here's the stylish shopper for the real romantic! A smart Tote Bag in natural canvas with the Mills & Boon red rose motif adding that extra touch of chic. Remember, it's yours to keep whether or not you become a subscriber.

where and when *he* wanted. He was that type of man
—indeed, he was the type of man she had always taken
care to avoid. She enjoyed her independence, made her
own decisions, fought her own battles.

As always when she met Sally Dalton, she immediately thought of Paul. She waved to Sally, then parked
neatly, rummaging around for her art materials as Sally
came running over.

Tudor Ward was quiet, as wards are at weekends.
Only essential nursing chores would be carried out.
There was open visiting on the ward, but visitors generally waited until the afternoon or evening, according to
the Junior Sister in charge.

'Help yourself to whatever you need,' Sister offered.
'Sit with the patients and help them relax. It all helps.'

Julia thanked her, then ushered Sally into the ward
itself. Having made her plans in advance, she led Sally
towards Ted Baxter. He glanced up listlessly as they
arrived at his bedside, then ignored them.

Sally nibbled her lip, clearly unsure what to do next.
Her pleading expression spoke volumes, but Julia didn't
know if she could do much for the man, either. As Paul
said, he didn't want to relax and he didn't want to be
helped.

Taking a deep breath, she plunged in. 'Are you
interested in art, Mr Baxter? Painting and so on? Nurse
Dalton is keen to start classes for those who are.'

There was a lengthy silence, then she saw the barely
perceptible shake of his head. 'We'll leave it for now,
then. If you should change your mind, Nurse Dalton will
be around to help you,' she said gently.

They moved on to Mrs McFarland, Julia deep in
thought. Perhaps seeing the two of them out of uniform
he didn't fully appreciate that they were nurses. She'd

given careful thought to the question of what they should wear. Since she wouldn't be coming very often, civvies were appropriate, but she suggested to Sally that she wore her first-year's uniform next time. The mauve and white striped material was distinctive, and with her plain paper cap she would stand out from the trained staff.

'Yes, Sister,' Sally sighed. 'If they're all like that man I can't see the project getting off the ground!'

'Don't be so easily discouraged,' Julia whispered. 'You can't expect success every time.'

Mrs McFarland was keen, though she confessed that she had no talent for anything. 'Nonsense,' Julia said kindly. 'You can probably whip up a good meal from next to nothing. That's a talent.'

'I suppose it is, Sister. I hadn't thought,' she agreed. 'That's a pretty colour,' she went on, indicating Julia's dress. 'Not often you find redheads wearing lilac.'

'That's probably because it clashes with red hair!' Julia smiled. 'It's one of my favourite colours, though.'

She wore her abundant, gleaming red-gold hair in its accustomed chignon and no jewellery except gold stud ear-rings and her wedding ring. On duty she did not wear the ring, and it was the first thing Rob Morland noticed when he strode into the ward some half-hour later. Julia saw his eyes gravitate to it as though they'd been pulled by a magnet, and she hoped he understood she was a widow. She didn't want him to think she was married yet still accepting invitations to dine out with eligible men. She wasn't Linda Greene.

The Registrar was casually dressed in stone-washed jeans and an equally faded blue shirt, and Sally also wore jeans and a cheesecloth overblouse. Julia felt over-dressed by comparison. Sally went bright red when Julia made the introductions. Clearly the Registrar had at least *one* fan! He was goodnatured with an easy charm that broke susceptible hearts, and she hoped Sally wouldn't make the mistake of falling for him. Paul Konrad would blame her if Sally suffered a broken heart, that was for sure.

Rob's eyes, at the moment, were expressing his silent admiration of *her* rather than Sally, and she wasn't sure if she should be pleased or sorry. A simple friendship was all she asked, but she knew that for most men it wasn't enough.

When Rob arrived, Sally had just finished sketching Mrs McFarland, who posed willingly. He duly admired the drawing, then kissed Mrs McFarland on the brow. 'The new Mona Lisa, that's what you're going to be. Mona Lisa of St Crispin's!' he teased. A lady who would soon recover if Dr Morland had any say in the matter!

Julia borrowed the sketch to show to Mr Baxter, who refused to even open his eyes. He was a sad but not an impossible case, she knew. In the unit they tried to select the most suitable helper for each patient, and she wondered who had been allocated to this man. Usually the occupational therapists did the spadework, just listening to the patients and then eventually assisting them to come to terms with their illness and their problems. Many others were involved, and Julia had met some of them.

With him, it would be uphill all the way, the more so since he had virtually insisted on an operation. For some the bypass op conferred a certain status. Because public personalities had undergone open-heart surgery it was fashionable and would continue to be so as the operation became more generally available.

She sat beside him for a little while, idly watching Rob and Sally. He had taken her under his wing, and Julia felt she could concentrate on Mr Baxter for a while. Of course he needed rest, and she must not deny him that, but he wouldn't be disturbed by her simply sitting there. On another visit, she decided she would sketch him even if he didn't willingly pose for her.

She sat there, idly sketching Sally from memory, and was pleased with the result. Out of the corner of her eyes, she caught a flicker of movement as Ted Baxter eased his body round in the bed, curious to know what she was doing. She didn't acknowledge his interest, afraid he would withdraw into his shell of misery again. When she finished with Sally she immediately began on a new sketch of Paul Konrad. Then Rob approached and she hurriedly closed her pad. She couldn't let him see the resemblance between student and consultant, a resemblance he probably wouldn't notice otherwise.

'Good morning, Mr Baxter,' Rob said loudly, but the man pretended not to hear.

Julia shook her head at Rob. 'Let Mr Baxter rest, Doctor. He's very tired and I really must go.' She rose, tall and slender and unconsciously graceful in her movements.

'Mr Carr is a lucky man,' Rob Morland threw in casually as they rejoined Sally.

'I'm a widow,' Julia said quietly. 'I have no plans for plunging into another marriage,' she added, anxious not to encourage him.

'Nor have I!' he confessed. 'One divorce is enough!'

Her smile was tinged with sadness. 'I'm sorry. Were . . . Have you any children?'

He shook his head. 'Being married to a doctor is no fun, particularly a junior doctor. Consultants have an easier time of it.'

'Have we? I didn't know,' said a male voice from right

beside Julia, and she swung round, surprised to see Paul Konrad here on a Saturday.

Rob didn't appear put out at seeing his Chief. 'You know that's true, sir,' he said affably.

Paul's frown was as dark as his eyes as he said quietly: 'The buck stops here, Dr Morland. I have no one senior to whom I can turn.' Having delivered that rebuke, he went on: 'Have we had the results from Mr Dailey's blood test? I wanted to check.'

'No, sir. I expect the results on Monday.'

Sally came up then, her face alight with pleasure at seeing Dr Konrad. 'Uncle Paul! I didn't know you'd be here.' She smiled shyly at him, and Julia was touched at the girl's devotion.

The consultant merely nodded, his hard face giving nothing away. 'Hello, Sally. Have you had a good morning?'

Sally appeared satisfied with what she had achieved. They were standing in the narrow corridor between the ward and the office now, out of earshot of the patients and out of the view of most. Gatherings of medical and nursing staff tended to frighten the sick, as each patient assumed he or she was the interesting topic of discussion!

'Mr Dailey isn't for an operation, is he?' asked Julia. 'He seems rather frail.'

'Too frail for surgery, I think,' Dr Konrad agreed, as they strolled through the now empty occupational therapy room. 'We have to consider whether surgery of *any* kind will give him extra years of life—life that is free from pain,' he emphasised. They paused by the door before going their separate ways, Julia reluctant to leave. She could listen to Paul talk all night, if need be. 'We must try to enhance the patient's life, to improve its quality,' he went on. 'If we merely lengthen it without making it more bearable then we have done someone a disservice.'

Julia found herself nodding in agreement. What use was a longer span of years if those years were spent in pain or in constant dread of overworking the already damaged heart? All these factors had to be weighed up and balanced. No operation and no treatment just for the sake of it.

'Now.' Dr Konrad turned to his Registrar. 'There is a job you can do for me. Dr Neale has the keys to the Medical Records Office. I need more information on Ted Baxter. His notes aren't complete and there should be a previous file on him somewhere.'

'Me, sir?' The Registrar sounded wary yet resigned, and Julia felt for him.

Paul frowned. 'I was going to search for the file, but as you are here . . .' He paused significantly. 'You were telling Sister Carr how hard junior doctors work. Now is your chance to prove it.'

'Yes, sir.' Rob threw Julia a weak smile. 'Sorry, ladies—duty calls! I'll treat you another time.'

'Oh, was he going to take us for coffee?' asked Sally when Rob left.

'No. Lunch,' Julia said shortly, giving the consultant a disapproving look.

He met her gaze blandly. 'In that case I have saved him some money. As well as being overworked, Dr Morland is underpaid,' he said, a glimmer of humour showing in his eyes.

She couldn't prevent herself from returning the smile and they stood there in a world of their own. Sally Dalton was temporarily forgotten until she plucked at the consultant's sleeve.

He gazèd down at the girl in surprise. Then Sally gave him that little smile that was so reminiscent of his own, and Julia turned swiftly away, unable to bear the pain. He, Sally and Rowena Dalton were a family, and she had no right to monopolise the man.

'I'll be off, then, Nurse,' she said briskly, making for the car park as quickly as she decently could. Her eyes were sore and there was a lump in her throat. She must be coming down with one of those summer colds that hang on and on—a summer cold that might well last for the two years of Paul's stay in England.

She was at her car when he came hurrying across to her, Sally in tow. 'I was about to offer you a lift home, Sister, but I see you have your own transport.' He stopped, then frowned at her car as though it had caused him some annoyance.

'Thank you, Doctor,' she said quietly, 'but I'll need my car on Monday morning. What about you, Nurse? I expect you're staying at the hospital?'

Sally, it transpired, was expected home for the rest of the day. 'It's a pity. We could have had lunch with Dr Morland,' the girl said wistfully.

'I'm sure there will be other occasions,' the consultant put in smoothly. 'I will drop Sally at home, Sister,' he added.

'Will you be staying to lunch?' asked Sally, before they moved away. 'Mother says you're taking her out tomorrow.'

Julia tried not to listen, but could perhaps have tried harder. There was silence for a few seconds, then she heard him tell Sally he had other plans for lunch. The two of them moved out of earshot, and Julia immediately wondered if his plans for lunch included Linda Greene.

It was mean of him to deprive her of lunch with the Registrar, and she was tempted to make her way to Medical Records and wait until Rob finished his search. It would serve Dr Konrad right if she did. His assistant was entitled to his weekend off.

It wasn't until she was nearly home that she realised she was being followed. Paul Konrad's sleek silver Mercedes was keeping a respectable distance behind. She supposed he would be turning off on to the Brighton road, which was just coming up, but to her surprise he ignored the turning, then slowed to let another car overtake. Wherever he was going he was in no hurry. He could easily have kept the overtaking car at bay.

The absurd thought crossed her mind that he was coming home with her! It was quite ridiculous. Yet the feeling wouldn't go away, and she wasn't all that surprised when the Mercedes eased its long body into the narrow driveway of the flats a few moments after her own arrival.

'Have you lost your way, Doctor?' She raised a brow enquiringly, as he glanced about him with exaggerated astonishment.

'I was on my way to lunch at the Harlequin,' he explained, 'but I decided to take a detour. Put your car in the garage and I'll take you out to lunch,' he added commandingly.

'I haven't a garage. These,' Julia pointed to the block of garages tucked away behind the house, 'are all taken.' Unless someone moves out I can't have one.'

'Who owns the house? I assumed it was hospital property,' he said once they were on their way.

She shook her head. 'No. It belongs to a big company. They're out on the industrial estate and without providing at least temporary accommodation they can't get suitable managers. They let me rent a flat, but if there's an influx of managers I'll have to go.'

'Oh? Are you a friend of the owners?' His voice was sharp with suspicion and, perversely, Julia decided not to enlighten him.

'Sort of,' she shrugged instead. He kept his private life from her, offered no explanations, so why should she be expected to bare all? It was none of his business.

The Harlequin was doing a roaring trade, but they were immediately shown to a corner table bearing a 'Reserved' sign. Julia's expression was thoughtful. 'You were expected, then?' She kept her voice light.

'So it would seem,' he agreed, his smile benign but giving nothing away. His dark eyes held hers for a moment and, confused, she hastily picked up the menu.

She refused a drink but could not resist the crisp, warm French bread when it was placed on their table. 'Mm, I'm being spoilt,' she smiled, taking a delicate bite of the bread which she had liberally spread with butter.

Paul was silent until the main course arrived. 'It doesn't sound as if you get many treats, Julia.' His tone was bland. So was his expression when she raised her eyes to his.

She shrugged, then smiled nonchalantly, endeavouring to convey the impression that she was always dining out. 'This is my second invitation to lunch today,' she pointed out. 'Dr Morland might have brought me here.'

'Yes, that's true,' he agreed mildly—so mildly that she wanted to shake him out of his complacency.

'He's good for me,' she went on, before finishing the last piece of chicken Marengo. 'He's fun—full of life,' she added for good measure, then helped herself to more bread. Being one of those naturally slender people who could eat anything and not gain weight, she intended to make the most of her lunch. It would probably be sardines on toast for dinner, since she didn't bother much when she was alone.

'Yes, so I believe,' Paul agreed. 'A most popular young man with the ladies.'

'I imagine so.' Julia smiled sweetly at him, then flushed as she realised he was laughing at her. He knew quite well she was trying to stir him up!

Determined to change the subject, she told him about Sally's morning in the unit.

'Ah, yes, the unit. And has she decided she will now become an artist?'

'I don't think she knows *what* she wants,' Julia offered, and he nodded.

'Rowena is keen that she should help me. But I'm not sure it is a good thing.'

'Yes, so she said,' Julia said carefully, then smiled at the waiter and ordered a vanilla ice.

'When did she say that?' His voice was sharp, and she wavered. He obviously didn't know about Mrs Dalton's unexpected visit.

'Oh, aren't you having a pudding?' she asked, trying to deflect his question. 'I can't recall when she said that. Probably at Sally's interview. Why don't you have an ice-cream too?' she hurried on.

'Julia, I do not wish for an ice-cream,' he said severely. 'Truth would be a better accompaniment to the meal.'

Julia looked at him. 'I honestly do not remember when Mrs Dalton mentioned that she wanted Sally to help you,' she lied. Her ice-cream arrived and she ate it defiantly. 'Thank you for the meal, Doctor. It was delicious, but I could have done without the post-mortem!' she hissed.

'For a post-mortem there needs to be a body. And I have not shaken Rowena to death—yet,' he said grimly.

Surprise held her silent, then a glimmer of hope dawned. Was all the affection on Rowena's side? Probably she was doing the hunting. Well, if she was, she had a wary prey. Dr Paul Konrad would not be captured without a fight!

She refused coffee, not wanting to prolong the meal. He might ask her more questions she would prefer not to answer. Afterwards, he drove off in the opposite direction to her flat and she demanded to know where they were going.

'I have seen your home. I thought you might wish to see mine,' he said, slowing the car as if waiting for her acquiescence before proceeding.

'Yes, I'd like that,' she agreed readily. 'Have you a flat or a whole house to yourself?'

'It's one floor only. A bungalow, but a big one.'

'We had a bungalow,' she said, almost to herself. It was small and neat but plenty big enough for the two of them. She pictured it still sometimes, though she had never driven past it since her move. It would be too poignant seeing another woman's curtains at her windows, another man's car in her drive. She closed her eyes momentarily, willing the last few years to be a nightmare from which she would surely soon awaken.

Glancing at the dark man sitting silently by her side, she knew that it was no dream. John lived on only in her memories. Tears welled up behind her eyes, but she successfully kept them under control. The man was taking the trouble to show her his home, reveal part of his private life. He didn't want a weepy woman spoiling his homecoming.

CHAPTER SEVEN

PAUL's home delighted Julia, although it was totally unlike her own. The bungalow sprawled across a generous-sized overgrown garden. The air was full of the scent of flowers as he inched the car along the badly-gravelled drive. 'It needs a lot of work done on it,' he commented.

'Oh, no, it doesn't!' she exclaimed. 'It's lovely the way it is. And what gorgeous views!' She gazed entranced at the magnificent view the property commanded. On the other side of the road farmland stretched away right up to the foot of the South Downs. They were so close to the Downs that she could see sheep grazing there. A horse, disturbed by the noise of the car, peered over the fence on the opposite side of the road.

'There's a riding stables not far away,' Paul told her. 'I like to ride when I can—though that isn't often enough.'

'Apart from seaside pony rides I've never been that close to a horse!' she confessed, and his soft laughter warmed her. It was natural for him to take her hand, leading her carefully across obstacles in the wild garden.

Part of the garden was very wild indeed, with flowering grasses standing knee-high. Everywhere the bees were busy, and Julia caught a flash of colour as butterflies glided delicately past before alighting on the abundance of blossoms. In the shelter of the dilapidated wall there was a small rock garden, and she couldn't resist a closer inspection. She did so miss her garden, and disliked having to make do with a windowbox and a few pots of cyclamen. The white alyssum had almost taken over the rock garden, but in between she saw thrift and a tiny form of columbine.

'I ought to have a gardener,' Paul acknowledged, 'but I would like to tame the garden in my own time. And in my own way,' he added. 'Here we are.' He unlocked the front door, which looked new, and ushered her into the surprisingly spacious interior.

'So often bungalows are little boxes intended for one old couple, but this is something else,' Julia said wonderingly. Without waiting for an invitation, she wandered around the bungalow. She came first to a long but narrow kitchen with its own breakfast bar tucked into a corner. It was freshly painted and had been fitted out recently, with neat floor and wall units in dazzling scarlet with white trim. The window overlooked the rear garden, which wasn't as big as the front and sides. It consisted mainly of lawn, newly-mowed, with a few fruit trees right at the bottom. An old potting shed leaned nonchalantly against a sagging fence, which divided the property from the chalet next door.

'The shed looks drunk,' she commented, as Paul joined her. 'So does the fence, for that matter!'

'It's the children next door. The place is owned by an old couple, but their grandchildren keep coming. They think it's great fun to clamber up the fence.'

'And you don't object?' Julia half turned, wondering at this unexpectedly genial side to his nature.

'I didn't particularly enjoy my childhood, and I like children,' he said shortly. 'I'll make us some coffee while you explore,' he added, his face closed and expressionless once more.

Sad that she'd hurt him, she made a brief inspection of the rest. The bungalow boasted three bedrooms, though none of them were large. A double bed was squeezed into the biggest bedroom, and, together with a massive wardrobe and chest of drawers, completely filled the room. The other two bedrooms had single beds, though neither was made up. In all three, the walls were covered in a pale pink embossed paper which looked like silk. It felt like silk, too, as Julia discovered, unable to resist touching.

The bathroom was in the process of being retiled, the new tiles being a deep pink with silver scrolls, and she wondered if Paul was a do-it-yourself man. Her face softened at the thought of him spending his free time in jeans and old sweater doing odd jobs, making the place fit to bring his bride. There was something endearing in the idea of the eminent specialist doing manual work, creating something with his own hands, stamping his personality upon the bungalow even if it was only for two years. Probably it was a kind of therapy, a way of unwinding after a hard day taking life-or-death decisions.

The main room was a front-facing sitting-room with a small dining recess. A mahogany dining table and chairs filled the recess, but the remainder of the room was sparsely furnished. A big squashy settee reposed under the window with two matching armchairs. An occasional table and a low cabinet were the only other items except for a white portable television on the cabinet. There were no flowers, no ornaments or pictures—nothing at all to suggest that a woman might live here. No photograph of Paul's wife. But then Julia did not display John's photo, either. For both of them, memories were private, intimate things and did not need a public display of grief or umpteen photographs of the dead everywhere.

Lost in her reverie, she didn't at first see Paul. He lounged in the doorway, dark eyes watchful, serious.

'Thank you for letting me roam over your home,' she said quietly. 'I've enjoyed it.'

He nodded curtly. 'Coffee's ready in the kitchen.'

When he suggested they took their coffee outside, Julia readily agreed. The garden fascinated her. Who knew what secrets lurked in its untamed beauty? She followed him around the side of the house where a derelict sun-lounge afforded some respite from the breeze.

He nodded towards the garden. 'I've made a start clearing it, but I wanted to let some of its wildness remain.'

'It's the sort of garden I would have liked,' she found herself saying. 'We had just a small patch of garden front and back. Not big enough to grow anything in, I'm afraid. You could grow your own vegetables once you get settled, couldn't you?'

'A lovely thought, but in two years' time . . .' Paul let the sentence trail away. 'I hope to get a dog soon,' he added. 'That's something I will not need to leave behind me. A home isn't complete without a dog.'

'That's what I . . .' she began, then laughed self-consciously. At this rate he would believe she was chasing him! First she told him his bungalow was delightful, then his garden was the sort she would have liked. Now she had been about to confess that she had always wanted a dog. He would be incredibly thick if he didn't get such an obvious message, though of course she hadn't meant it that way. It was just that they had so much in common; they were like minds. And that hurt more than anything.

She lingered over the coffee as long as she could, strangely reluctant to leave Paul's home. Here peace and tranquillity reigned. Although the road in front of the property was busy, the front garden was so big that traffic sounds were muted, and already she found she could ignore them. The world held only the two of them, and she could not remember when she had last known such utter peace. She leaned back in the deckchair and closed her eyes. This was paradise, albeit a temporary one.

She didn't know what woke her. Perhaps it was the sudden movement of a bird in the undergrowth, or some tiny wild creature. She sat up, feeling ashamed of sleeping in someone else's garden. Paul's eyes were on her face and there was a depth of sadness there that alarmed her. It was as if he was already gone from her, had left her forever. Warning bells rang in her head as she tried to brush aside the eerie feeling.

'What is it, Paul?' she whispered. Somehow it seemed wrong to speak normally, to break the silence.

'You spoke in your sleep,' he said stonily, getting up and standing with his broad back to her. 'You called "John".' He swung round. 'Does he still mean so much to you?'

'Why, of course he does.' Her voice was shaky. 'Though I don't spend a lot of time thinking about him now. It's only sometimes . . . A memory returns or I see or hear something . . . a favourite tune, or a flower,' she went on, slowly, painfully. 'Or your tweed jacket. He liked tweed.' When he didn't comment, she went on: 'Your bungalow, too. Oh, it's nothing like the one we had, but it brought back memories. And the dog. We were going to buy a dog once I gave up work. We . . .' No, she couldn't tell him about the baby they had planned. What business was it of his, anyway? His future lay with Rowena Dalton.

With a determined air, she got up. No good would come of brooding on the past. The next chance she got to go out with the new Registrar she would take. *He* wouldn't encourage her in morbid reflections. Tears weren't far away as she thanked him for the coffee. 'And for the grand tour!' she laughed. Then to her horror the laughter became mingled with tears. She found her wet face being cradled in strong, bronzed hands, her tears being kissed away as rapidly as they fell.

'My Julia,' Paul murmured huskily, as she laid her head thankfully upon his chest. He began to stroke her hair, and she clung to him as sobs racked her slender frame. 'Cry, Julia! It is for the best,' he commanded, but she needed no telling. Indeed, it was difficult to stop. She closed her tired eyes, content to listen to his calm tones.

Eventually the tears dried. Ashamed of her break-down, Julia raised her tear-stained face to his and he pressed his lips on hers. Smiling tremulously, she tried to speak, to thank him for his patience and understanding, but no words came. She felt his fingers at her hair, gently loosening her chignon. Wild red hair tumbled about her as he skilfully removed the pins. 'Such beautiful hair,' he murmured.

'It isn't beautiful n-now,' she croaked. 'You'll have to lend me a comb—I must look awful. I *feel* a mess, anyway!'

'You still look lovely,' he said once they were indoors. 'It is a pity you cannot sketch yourself. You have a great deal of talent.'

Carefully Julia ran his comb through her hair, then rinsed her face. They were in the bathroom, and she thankfully patted her heated face dry on a soft beige towel. 'You know about the drawings.' It was a statement rather than a question and she didn't need his nod of assent.

'Your charming Principal Tutor mentioned them— casually, of course.'

'Of course,' she echoed, ashamed of the trouble she might have caused him. 'It was just that—I found myself sketching Nurse Dalton and——'

'And inevitably you noticed a resemblance,' he said heavily.

'Yes,' she admitted bleakly, then busied herself drawing back her hair with grips, ready to put it up again.

His hand on her arm restrained her. 'No, leave it. Such lovely hair should not be bundled out of sight,' he said sharply.

Too drained to argue, Julia let her hair fall, and Paul gently stroked it. She tensed, afraid he wanted to make love. Whatever happened she mustn't encourage him —for it was what she wanted, too. She was honest enough to acknowledge the fact, but only to herself. He must never know how much her body longed for him, how her senses clamoured for release, how she loved him . . . Shocked at the idea of loving him, she jerked herself free. What nonsense! Of course she didn't love him. It was purely animal attraction.

'I'm very sorry about the drawings, Paul. I left them locked in my drawer in the office, but I was late arriving last Monday and my colleague, Sister Hamilton, went to the drawer. She isn't a gossip and I know she wouldn't have told anyone, but the Principal Tutor saw them, too. The rest you know,' she said wearily. She turned big, deep blue eyes on him, gazing up earnestly into his face, willing him to understand how sorry she was. 'Did she say anything to you? Remark on the likeness? No, I suppose she wouldn't.' It would hardly be her boss's place to remark on a likeness between consultant and student nurse.

'She made no comment,' he agreed. 'But she fixed me with a look!' Surprisingly, there was dry humour in his voice, and Julia could imagine the scene.

'She's good at those. I don't know how to make amends, I——' She stopped and they both heard the sound of tyres screeching on the path. 'You have a visitor, Paul,' she said, her smile uneven. Naturally it would be Rowena Dalton. Sally would have told her that the doctor had other plans for lunch, and the woman wasn't stupid.

Paul's brows met in an ominous frown. 'Who can——' he began, then they heard Mrs Dalton's voice calling through the letterbox.

'Who else but your lady love?' said Julia, trying to sound unconcerned. 'Sally must have told her you met me on the ward. Naturally your fiancée has a right to know what you get up to behind her back. Thank you for the coffee.'

She hurried away before he could speak. Then she heard him call her name as she went to open the front door. It had occurred to her to slip out the back way, but she wouldn't sneak out like a thief in the night.

Head held proudly, she welcomed Rowena Dalton, whose dark eyes glittered at the surprising sight of the Senior Clinical Teacher with her hair down, looking as if she had just been kissed. 'I hope you have an enjoyable afternoon, Mrs Dalton,' Julia said sweetly. 'I've had a most enjoyable morning,' she added rashly. It was bitchy perhaps, but in the circumstances she felt it was wholly justified.

Her head ached, so did her heart, and by the time she had trekked to the nearest phone-box to ring for a taxi, so would her feet. She'd had enough of them both for one day!

Julia didn't see Paul Konrad again until Tuesday. When they met, she was talking to the irrepressible Rob Morland on Tudor Ward.

'We're both running in the marathon the weekend after next,' Rob told her firmly.

'I can't run,' she protested weakly, knowing she would capitulate. It might be rather fun, and it would be for a good cause.

'With those long legs it shouldn't be difficult,' Rob pointed out as he scribbled her name down on his pad. 'Right, that's another victim!'

'Will there be many of us?' Against her will, she wondered if Paul was also taking part.

'Quite a few, but don't worry about the others. I shall be by your side! Anyway, it's not exactly a run, more of a sponsored fast walk. Family affair, children, dogs, etc!'

Smiling despite herself, Julia was about to joke about it, then became aware of the consultant a few feet away.

'I wanted a word with you, Sister, if you please,' said Paul, his cool gaze resting on them both.

Evidently not realising his presence wasn't wanted, Rob Morland stuck his ground, and this seemed to irritate Paul, for he glowered. He had a most unpredictable temper, and Julia was glad that for once she wasn't the victim of his variable moods.

'You wanted your students to sit in on my outpatient clinics,' he began, and she nodded, delighted.

'Yes, please! Can you find room for one now?'

To her surprise, he said he would allow two students

to sit in on his clinics. 'For a trial period only,' he warned. 'If they become a nuisance, they go!' He made a chopping motion with his hand. Julia's eyes widened. He really *was* in a mood! Never mind, she must humour the man, show her gratitude for his kindness.

'That's most kind of——' she began, but he was already striding away, and she turned her startled gaze on the Registrar.

'He's in one hell of a mood,' he commented. 'I can't do a thing right!'

Puzzled, she continued through to the ward. Mr Baxter was about the same. He was awake, but appeared not to recognise Julia at first.

She laid her cool hand on his brow. 'Are you responding to treatment, Mr Baxter?' she asked crisply, 'or fighting it?'

'I feel so tired,' he muttered, his eyes less apathetic now. 'So tired.'

'What about visitors? Does anyone come?' She sat by his bed, realising that she must make the most of this opening.

'I'm a widower. Got no family.'

'Friends from work, then?'

There was no reply to that question, and Julia sat there a while longer, not wanting to rush away. She intended mentioning the question of visitors to Sister Greene. She had no doubt that the matter had been fully investigated and that she would be accused of interfering, but she couldn't sit back and do nothing. No more conversation was forthcoming, and she rose to go just as the consultant and his assistant walked into the ward.

She eyed Paul warily. Of course he would not take her to task on the ward, but after Saturday he wasn't her favourite person, and she wasn't sure she could be civil to him if he snapped at her again.

Her antipathy towards him must have shown in her face, for he smiled lazily, completely throwing her off balance. She couldn't glare at him in front of Rob, so she returned the smile as best she could.

'Will you be visiting the ward next Saturday?' he enquired, his voice bland.

'I . . . I'm not sure,' she wavered, then recalled that Rob Morland would be on duty. 'Yes, I think I may, Doctor.'

Rob smiled at her behind his Chief's back. She *would* come on Saturday. It would give her a chance to see the Registrar again and have a chat with Mr Baxter. Remembering Mr Baxter, she turned for a last glance at him, but he appeared to be sleeping.

'He needs rest, Julia,' murmured Paul, and she saw the flicker of surprise that crossed Rob's face.

'I asked if he had any visitors, but he says he hasn't anyone. Is there no one at all?' she asked quietly, Dr Morland forgotten.

Paul frowned. 'There's a stepdaughter, but she lives in the Midlands somewhere—he doesn't know where, and we had to prise even that amount of information out of him. We've allocated Nurse Black to him, but she's finding it hard going.' He paused. 'Perhaps you could help in his rehabilitation? Yes, you must help. I will arrange it with Sister Greene,' he said decisively, before she could protest. 'I will walk back a little way with you. Carry on here, Dr Morland.'

'Yes, sir.' The Registrar sounded resigned, and he and Julia exchanged perplexed glances as she obediently followed Paul from the ward. He was like a chameleon, and it was all rather trying.

'I never know where I am with you!' she protested, once they were in the corridor. 'Blow hot, blow cold —that's you!'

'It's your climate,' he said, with a hint of a smile.

Julia watched his beautifully-shaped mouth arrange itself into a proper smile, and could not be annoyed with him any more. If only she didn't care for him! It was all so unfair.

His eyes were quizzical. 'No sharp retort, my Julia?'

'No!' she snapped, her good intentions vanishing. 'And don't call me your Julia! I'm not.'

'You could be.' His voice was sensuous, so was his expression, and a swift tide of colour crept up her face before she could walk away.

'You embarrass me, Dr Konrad.' She tried to look fierce but couldn't manage it, and his smile broadened.

'Poor Julia! You don't know whether to embrace me or kick me in the teeth!'

She chuckled. 'Don't tempt me, Doctor! I have a fierce temper once I get going.'

'It's a sign of a passionate nature. Or so I am told,' he said silkily.

She decided to let that pass. His passionate nature was Rowena Dalton's concern.

There was a significant pause, then he said abruptly: 'I wish to apologise for Saturday, Julia. There was no need for you to go.'

'Three's a crowd. I didn't think Mrs Dalton would welcome my presence. If you're going to marry the woman——'

'There is no question of marriage!' he snapped. 'The idea is Rowena's, not mine.'

'If you're lovers I suppose it's only natural she should

think of marriage.' Julia forced the words out through dry lips. She wasn't asking him to confirm or deny the charge. She didn't want to know the truth. Yet wouldn't that be better than not knowing?

'First I am Sally's father,' he snapped in exasperation, 'now I am Rowena's current lover. If these accusations are both true, it isn't likely I will marry her after all these years. Is it?' he demanded, and Julia shook her head. Put like that, it wasn't logical.

'You might have met again after a long absence,' she suggested, and his face darkened with rage.

'I would like to shake you until your brain rattles!' he gritted fiercely. 'If you have a brain!' he added.

'Just you listen to me, Paul Konrad——!' she began, but to her chagrin he walked away, and she was left staring after him in futile anger. Her eyes followed his tall, proud figure until he was out of sight. Oh, Paul! her heart cried. Why do we keep quarrelling? They were too much alike, that was why. Opposites attract; everyone knew that. It simply wasn't possible for the pair of them to get on well, to live or work together for any length of time without quarrelling. Mother Nature had slipped up there!

The following afternoon, she had some free time and slipped into Tudor to see Ted Baxter again. This time there was no response to her conversation, though Rob Morland told her there was a definite improvement in the man's heart condition.

'He gets angina only on exertion and there's no reason for him to exert himself here,' said Rob as they sat in the office. Sister Greene was at tea, and Julia had purposely timed her visit in order to miss her. 'Of course we don't let him lie in bed all day—that's no treatment. Whenever he's asked to do simple exercises, though, he complains of cardiac pain. "It's like a tight band around my chest, Doctor", he keeps saying.'

'And is it a real pain?' asked Julia, thinking it could be psychosomatic.

'He suffers a real pain, yes,' Rob conceded, 'but his nervous state brings it on. He's so convinced that exertion will bring pain that it does. I think he should either go to another ward or be transferred for surgery. I keep telling the Old Man there's nothing we can do for him here.'

'I take it that you mean Dr Konrad?' she smiled, her eyes dancing at the idea of Paul being called an old man, though it was a term junior doctors often used to describe their consultant.

'Do you fancy him, Julia?'

Taken aback by the bluntness of the question, Julia was about to prevaricate, then she saw Linda Greene in the doorway, her sharp ears also keen to know the truth.

'I was afraid I might miss you,' Julia said sweetly. 'I just popped in to see Mr Baxter, but he's staring into space and being unco-operative.'

Linda shrugged. 'I've told Paul there isn't anything we can do, but he just glowers at me.'

'I thought I was the only nurse he glowered at,' Julia sighed. 'I seem to upset the man without even trying.'

'We've all fallen victim to his black moods,' Rob put in, his cheerful face glum for once. 'He must have a lot of problems.'

'He has. And talking about him behind his back isn't exactly professional, Dr Morland!' Sister Greene said firmly, her censorious gaze including Julia in the reproof. 'I hear you're taking Mr Baxter over,' she added, this time addressing Julia directly.

'No, I'm not,' Julia disclaimed quickly. 'He needs

constant counselling and I have my own job to do. I thought I could provide a little extra interest for him, that was all.'

'Paul made it sound as if you were going to cure the poor man,' grumbled Linda. 'And what about the art therapy? Is Sally going to continue with that? It isn't something she can pick up and put down whenever the fancy takes her!'

Julia recognised the truth in that. Sally was rather dilatory, she felt, and the Tudor patients must not be allowed to suffer because of it. 'I'm sure Nurse Dalton will come whenever she can, Linda. If she shows signs of flagging or has a lot of extra studying to do, I'll take over,' she promised, wondering how she could get Paul's permission.

There was a visitor waiting for her when she arrived home, rather later than usual. At first she didn't recognise the tall, rather obese man who greeted her warmly, then her face cleared as the man moved away from the brand-new Rover. It was Mr Randolph, her landlord.

'It's been a long time, Mr Randolph!' she said warmly, clasping his outstretched hand. 'You've put on weight,' she added.

He frowned, then gave a short laugh. 'I was about to reprimand you, Sister! Then I remembered your profession. You're quite right, I *am* a trifle stout,' he agreed as he followed her up the stairs. She was alarmed at the noise his breathing made and wondered if he would make it to her flat. He was a candidate for a myocardial infarction, if ever she saw one.

'This is very cosy, Sister. Ah yes, tea. Two sugars,' he wheezed, once she'd got him sitting down. She hoped he would sit quietly while she made the tea in the small kitchen, but he followed her.

'I've seen the other tenants, Sister, and was about to leave. I thought perhaps you were working a late duty,' he explained. 'The wife isn't too well now, you know —gets these chest pains.'

'I hope she's seen her doctor. Chest pains need investigating, Mr Randolph. They won't go away without treatment,' Julia warned.

He mopped his brow, leaning against the door jamb. 'I get them, too, but I've got these marvellous tablets. They dissolve under the——Ah!'

Before Julia could speak, he clutched at his chest and swayed gently. She was just in time to support him or he would have fallen. As it was she had some two hundred pounds of elderly man to prop up, but managed to lean him against the door again, while she searched his pockets for the tablets to place under his tongue.

'It's the pain again,' he mumbled. 'In my waistc . . .' Her searching fingers closed round the tablets just as he collapsed against her with a groan, effectively wedging her in the doorway. Her flat bell rang at that moment.

CHAPTER EIGHT

EVENTS moved quickly after that, though Julia was to remember the nightmare situation for a long time to come.

She doubted if the person at the door would hear her, but she shouted anyway, calling for an ambulance at the top of her voice. Time was of the essence. Even seconds were vital, but they ticked steadily away as she managed to squeeze past Mr Randolph, then eased him to the floor, falling with him and taking his weight as they fell. It was difficult escaping from under his inert form, but desperation lent her strength she did not know she possessed.

She felt for a heartbeat, but there was none, and because it was important to get oxygen to his brain, she began mouth-to-mouth resuscitation. Those first few breaths might save his life, but somehow she doubted it. Then, wishing fervently that she had the telephone in, she rushed to the door to demand that her caller ring for an ambulance. There was no one there, and she almost sobbed in disappointment. 'Get an ambulance—cardiac arrest!' she screamed, then was rewarded by the sight of Paul Konrad bounding up the stairs.

She hurried back to Mr Randolph, closely followed by Paul, and between them they carried on with the resuscitation.

'Ambulance is on its way,' Paul told her in a brief pause.

Then the flat was full as the ambulance men arrived,

equipment at the ready. She and Paul accompanied her landlord in the ambulance, while resuscitation measures continued, but she knew from Paul's face that it was in vain.

Mr Randolph was pronounced dead shortly after arrival at St Crispin's, and once Julia had given the relevant details, she left, she and Paul returning to her flat in a taxi. She felt she ought to be there when Mrs Randolph was told, but Paul vetoed the idea when she mentioned it.

'Far better to rest a little first. *You* haven't recovered from the shock, so how can you help her?'

There was sense in what he said, so Julia reluctantly accompanied him back to the flat. Unusually docile, she sipped the tea he provided and nibbled a sweet biscuit, though after such an emergency she had no appetite. It was a long time since lunch, though, and she had to keep her strength up if she was later going to console Mrs Randolph.

'How did you guess it was a cardiac arrest?' she asked, suddenly recalling his remark about calling an ambulance for cardiac arrest.

'I heard you yelling for an ambulance and fortunately there was someone in the first flat I tried,' he explained, his gaze grave and troubled. 'A young woman told me the landlord had called and that he'd probably had a heart attack. He was grossly overweight. I'm surprised he made the journey to your flat,' he went on, frowning at her. 'A letter would have been sufficient, surely?'

She was too weary to argue with him, but the implication was obvious—Mr Randolph had an ulterior motive for his visit. 'He obviously wanted to see me in person,' she said quietly. 'Perhaps he's got a tenant for this flat. Oh, dear!' She would have to leave. During long winter nights she often lay awake listening to the old house groaning, or the antiquated central heating 'clinking' at intervals—weird noises but homely ones. Poor Mr Randolph, and poor old house.

If Paul wondered how she came to be given a flat intended for one of Mr Randolph's employees, he did not comment on it, and for that she was grateful.

Later, he drove her to see Mrs Randolph. She was resting, her doctor having prescribed an anxiolytic drug, and the meeting wasn't as traumatic as Julia feared. Mrs Randolph appeared comforted to hear about her husband's last moments and to be reassured that he had not suffered. Nevertheless, Julia felt guilty because he had died visiting her. She should not have allowed him to climb all those stairs.

When she voiced her thoughts, Paul told her firmly that the man could have died any time. 'You cannot apportion blame, Julia,' he said soothingly. 'Call it an act of God.'

She was half asleep by the time they got back, and it was all she could do to mount what seemed thousands of stairs. She got no farther than stair number five, then the consultant swept her up in his arms and, despite her protests, carried her the rest of the way. She laid her weary head against the comforting protection of his shoulder and closed her eyes.

It was with reluctance that she relinquished her tight grip about his neck, as he gently lowered her on to the settee.

'That was a death grip, my Julia,' he chuckled. 'I thought you were trying to strangle me!'

'I'd like to, on occasions,' she said frankly. 'Thank you for your kindness. I . . . Oh! You didn't tell me why you came.' In all the trauma she hadn't thought to ask him. It was enough that he was there when she needed him.

'It was nothing of importance.' He stood over her, his expression thoughtful. 'I have a free evening, and a walk among your beautiful Downlands appealed to me. I hoped you would come.'

'I would have enjoyed that!' Her voice was too eager, she knew, but she was too tired for subterfuge. What was wrong with letting him know how keen she was on his company?

'When I have another evening free, I shall call for you,' he promised.

'Yes, that will be lovely.' Her tone was subdued. 'When he had another evening free' really meant when he could escape from Rowena Dalton for a few hours.

'Julia? What is it? Tell me,' he urged, sitting beside her.

'Please go, Paul.' Her voice was no more than a whisper. 'I'm so tired and upset I can't think straight.' She turned her face away, hoping he would take the hint and leave.

'Naturally,' he murmured soothingly, but instead of leaving, he drew her towards him, his arms strong and comforting. With a sigh, Julia snuggled up to him and closed her eyes. She could not fight him any more. Nor, indeed, did she want to.

He murmured soothing words in her ear, in what she supposed was his own language. Although she couldn't understand them, their repetition served to lull her to sleep.

When she awoke it was dark and she was in her own bed. She lay quietly for a moment as she tried to get her bearings. She could not remember getting into bed, nor could she recall undressing. Perplexed, she sat up, glancing around. She wasn't completely undressed and she still wore her undies and tights, but her uniform dress was missing. Throwing back the duvet, she felt around for the light switch, the bedroom not boasting a bedside lamp.

Yes, there was her white uniform dress draped neatly over the back of a chair, her duty shoes placed tidily underneath.

Just as she began to recall the traumatic events of the day, a sound disturbed her. An intruder! she thought in alarm. Perhaps she hadn't locked the flat door. Never a timid girl, she picked up one of her heavy shoes and advanced upon the sitting-room, flinging back the door with a resounding crash.

Paul Konrad shot out of the best armchair, his hair tousled from sleep.

'Oh, it's you!' Julia muttered. The adrenalin was flowing along her veins as she prepared to do battle, and it was rather an anticlimax to find that there was no battle to fight. Feeling silly, she glanced down at her duty shoe. 'I thought you were a burglar,' she explained.

'He would be enjoying a rare sight right now,' he drawled, his gaze slowly travelling her body. 'It might have put him off stealing the family silver,' he added with a soft chuckle, and she fled.

Her bra, pants and slip were perfectly respectable, but still Paul had no right to inspect her quite so familiarly! Come to that, he had no right to remove her dress, for she certainly had no recollection of doing so. Her face burned, and she hated him for the embarrassment he'd caused her.

Safely enveloped in her dressing gown, she went back to the sitting-room, intending to give him a piece of her mind. She opened her mouth ready to nag him, but stopped in the doorway. Paul was asleep again, though the armchair must have been far from comfortable for such a large man. He had removed his jacket and tie, and his own shoes were parked neatly on the copper fender.

Even in sleep Paul Konrad did not relax. His face was hard and ruthless still, his eyes shut tight against the world. Julia suspected that like a wild animal, he slept with one ear alert for danger, and she wondered sadly what events in his past had caused him to be the way he was—a very private man, trusting no one, asking no quarter and giving none.

Her heart ached, as it did so often these days. She wanted to put her cool hand on his brow, smooth back that absurd lock of hair that kept getting in his eyes. And yes, she wanted to snuggle beside him, feel his body warming hers, his heart beating in unison with her own. Strange. It was like being in love, but how could she love the doctor from nowhere? She knew nothing about him. His relationship with Mrs Dalton was enough to place a barrier between them. Then there was Linda Greene . .

Besides, she told herself briskly, as she got back into bed, in two years he would be gone. Probably leaving behind a trail of broken hearts, she thought wryly, as she settled down to sleep, content in the knowledge that Paul would respect her privacy. Good job *my* heart isn't among them, she mused. At least, she hoped it wasn't.

By next morning it all seemed like a dream. Julia awoke early from sheer habit, trying to recall what day it was. It could not be Saturday because she knew she had not cleared her desk. In truth, she really didn't care. Never had she felt so tired, so bone-weary, not even on her spell of night duty. It must be age—only a short while until birthday number twenty-seven.

Suddenly she remembered Paul. She jumped out of bed, hardly daring to hope that he would still be in her armchair. No, of course he must have gone. His Mercedes parked out the front all night would cause both of them a lot of heartache. It would be all round the hospital in no time.

Yes, he was gone, leaving no trace that he had ever been there—not even a cup to indicate that he'd made himself a coffee before leaving. Julia began to believe she had imagined it all. Had he visited, put her to bed, soothed her fears? Or was it only her fevered imagination?

She forced herself to eat a slice of toast and marmalade, and take a few sips of coffee. It must have been a dream. Yet it was so real. Why, she had even spoken to him!

If anyone noticed that Sister Carr was rather odd that morning, no one commented, and she supposed she looked and behaved much the same as usual. She felt different, though. She was only half with her learners, the other half being with the cardiologist, wherever in the hospital he might be.

It was with some trepidation that she ventured on to Tudor that afternoon. Of course he wouldn't be there, but one could never be absolutely sure. He did not keep to specific round days, preferring to drop in unexpectedly, apart from the regular Friday morning case conference.

Student Nurse Neville was busy with a patient, so Julia paid a brief visit to Ted Baxter. There, too, she drew a blank, for he was sound asleep. She smiled to herself as she gazed at him. For him to enjoy a good sleep was a vast improvement. Tudor was doing him *some* good!

She was chatting to Mrs McFarland when she felt the disapproving gaze of Paul Konrad. She waved to him, and Mrs McFarland giggled. 'He looks in a mood, Sister. He was very grim this morning.'

'Oh? Perhaps he had a disturbed night,' Julia suggested, wondering what the patient would say if she had seen Paul Konrad sleeping in the armchair!

After checking Nurse Neville's work and asking if she had any problems, Julia drifted slowly towards the consultant, who was sitting in the office.

He glanced up as she hovered in the doorway. Sister Greene, fortunately, was nowhere in sight. 'About the mural, Doctor,' Julia said briskly.

His expression didn't change, though he must have been surprised. 'What mural, Sister Carr?'

'The mural Nurse Dalton is going to paint for the ward. I thought we might use the far wall where everyone can see it. Subject to your approval, naturally.'

'Naturally.' His tone was wry. 'I am surprised you troubled to consult me.'

Immediately she was on the defensive. 'I haven't mentioned it before because I thought you would disapprove. I hoped to help Nurse with the mural. They've got a beautiful one on Brer Rabbit. And in Casualty,' she added, hoping to sway him.

'*You* intend helping with the mural?'

'Yes, I do,' she said firmly. 'I would like to help, to do my bit for your patients. I know you don't want me to do art therapy on your ward!' she hurried on, irked by his attitude.

Impatiently he brushed her words aside. 'I didn't want you on Tudor at all, Sister Carr,' he said testily. 'You are a disturbing influence.'

Julia gasped at the unfairness of the charge. 'Just let

me tell you——' she began, but he wouldn't let her continue.

'Yet you have crept on to the ward,' he went on as if she hadn't spoken, 'doing things for my patients—and for me,' he added with a glimmer of a smile. 'Have your way. Paint your mural,' he finished abruptly, then strode away, leaving her shocked and shaken.

To be called a disturbing influence! What right had he to make such an accusation?

She didn't see Paul any more that week, which was just as well, since he caused her such heartache. The art therapy on Saturday went well, and Sally Dalton appeared as keen as ever. She was keener on the art than she was on nursing—that much was emerging.

Rob Morland was on duty over the weekend, and when he suggested Julia join him for a quiet supper after work, she accepted. It wasn't entirely fair to him but, after all, a supper date did not commit them to a torrid romance. Probably he was lonely. He was a Midlander and must be missing his friends and colleagues. She was being kind to a newcomer by accepting his invitation, that was all.

Whether Rob thought she was acting out of mere kindness was another matter. True, he kept the conversation light, not touching on intimate matters like his divorce or his hopes for the future. Once he stopped grinning and trying to be the life and soul of the party, he was an interesting companion. Julia liked this side of his nature, and told him so in her forthright manner.

'That's it—give it to 'em straight from the shoulder!' he quipped. 'Sorry, I'm being a clown again. Force of habit.' He crunched his bean-shoots noisily. 'I like Chinese food. Used to eat a lot of takeaways when I was training,' he told her.

'Mm, same here.' The Chinese restaurant was on the outskirts of the town, well away from the Harlequin. That was something to be thankful for, though Julia knew the takeaway food section was popular among the St Crispin's staff.

The restaurant was full and at first she couldn't see any of her colleagues. Then someone's blonde hair cuaght her eye and she was gazing admiringly at the long, silky hair and wishing she could be blonde, when she realised —she was staring at Linda Greene! She went pale, noticeably so, because Rob commented on it.

'Julia? Are you okay?'

Alarmed, she edged further over towards Rob, not wanting to be seen. Who would have thought that Paul would come here?

'Julia? Speak to me!' The Registrar's voice at last penetrated, and she focused on him.

'That's Sister Greene over there,' she said reluctantly. 'At least, I think it is.'

'Where? Oh, yes. Who's the bloke?'

'Don't you know . . . Isn't it someone from the hospital?' Curious now, she half rose. No, it wasn't Paul Konrad. It was Mike, Linda Greene's husband! Joy ran through her veins and she felt lightheaded as she smiled at Rob. 'It's Linda's husband. They must be together again. Isn't that nice?'

'Nice? Is it?' Rob's eyes met hers, and she hurriedly took a sip of wine.

'This is good. What is it?' She twirled the wineglass between her fingers, watching as the white wine sparkled in the light.

'It's a Riesling, if you're really interested.' Rob's tone was chilly.

'Rob!' Her glance was reproachful.

'You thought she was with old Blood-and-Thunder, didn't you?' he accused, and she shrugged.

'He wouldn't be flattered at that description. He isn't that hard to work for, is he?'

'No. He's not too bad,' he acknowledged. 'He's good at explaining things and doesn't automatically assume that I know everything. Better than some chiefs, really.' His tone was grudging and Julie didn't press him for more details. It was enough that Rob had bestowed *some* praise on Paul Konrad. It made her feel a lot happier, and she was in good spirits when they said goodnight. At her request, they had met in town, and she drove herself home. She wanted to avoid having to invite Rob in for coffee. There was no point in prolonging the evening, pleasant though it had proved.

What was even more pleasant was that Linda was back with her husband. They weren't snarling at each other as they'd done before, even in public. Nor did they give the impression that they were meeting only to divide up the furniture. They seemed happy together.

After a lonely Sunday Julia was glad to be back on duty on Monday. Of course she could have called in on Tudor Ward. Rob would have welcomed her, but there would be no Paul Konrad. She wondered how he had spent the day. Perhaps he had taken Rowena and her daughter for another Downland stroll.

Monday was as busy as usual, and Julia's mind was kept fully occupied. She didn't have time to even think about Paul until well into the afternoon, when she decided she would drop into Tudor. It was Student Nurse Neville's day off, but Mr Baxter ought to have a visit.

He was sitting in a chair with a sketchpad on his knees, and Julia's heart lifted at the welcome sight. On

Saturday he seemed better and was just starting to appreciate the art class, she felt.

'Hello, Mr Baxter,' she greeted him with a smile, which he almost returned. His mouth turned up a little at the corners, but it was better than nothing.

'Thought I might try my hand, Sister,' he muttered, his face returning to its usual gloomy lines.

She duly admired his work, which wasn't very good. It was progress, though, and she sat with him, encouraging him to practise.

His attacks of angina had ceased, he told her. 'Doctor says I don't need an op—says I'm a lot better,' he went on proudly, and Julia squeezed his hand.

'Doctor knows best,' she assured him. 'Why have a totally unnecessary operation if you can be cured simply by rest and graded exercises?'

'Bloke at the factory had the bypass operation—one of the managers. *He's* better for it. They had a big collection for him,' he went on dolefully.

Judging by the flowers at his bedside, Mr Baxter's colleagues hadn't entirely forgotten him. Julia mentioned his stepdaughter, but it was the wrong thing to say.

'She don't want anything to do with me,' he said abruptly, then closed his eyes and refused to say any more.

Then she saw Sister Greene bearing down upon her, followed by Paul. Now she would be blamed for upsetting Mr Baxter! In all honesty, she had to admit she was in the wrong. Yet if seeing the stepdaughter could assist him in making a full recovery, what was wrong with that? Something was preying on his mind, making him depressed, and it could be a family problem.

She got up. Paul greeted her distantly, though to her

amazement Linda smiled—a rare privilege! It must mean that she *was* back with her husband and this time they were happy.

She returned the smile, delighted for her colleague for more reasons than one.

The cardiologist settled himself in a chair beside Ted Baxter. 'How is the artwork coming on?' he asked, and Julia held her breath.

Mr Baxter cast him a reproachful look. 'Sister mentioned Irene—that's my stepdaughter.'

'How is she?'

'Dunno. Haven't seen her these fifteen years or more,' the patient said dolefully. Paul said nothing, and, after a lengthy pause, Mr Baxter went on: 'Do you think she'd want to see me after all these years? No, not after all this time.' He shook his head.

Paul reached for Mr Baxter's pulse. 'Your pulse is settling nicely. How do you feel about going home next week? I can follow you up weekly for a time.'

Mr Baxter blanched, then, as Julia might have expected, clutched at his chest. 'It's this pain, Doctor! Comes on something cruel, it does.' He grabbed Paul's hand. 'If I could have that op, the one the nobs have, I'd be a new man.'

'You will never be a new man,' Paul said deliberately. His voice was cold. 'You cannot escape from your own personality, your own failures.' He rose, austere and dignified. 'If you have made up your mind, I'll get my surgical colleague to assess you. Good afternoon.' He strode on to the next cubicle, Julia and Linda exchanging startled glances before the Ward Sister hurried after him.

Julia sat in the chair so abruptly vacated by the doctor. She took hold of the patient's hand but did not speak.

After Paul's bluntness it was for the patient to voice an opinion. She wouldn't have believed he could be so cruel! It contravened all she had learned in her own training and all she taught others. He had left the poor man defenceless, stripped him of all dignity, she felt. If Mr Baxter reported him, she wouldn't blame him.

'Doctor had no right to say them things,' Mr Baxter mumbled, and her heart bled for him.

'I'm sure he didn't mean to upset you,' she said comfortingly.

'I've got Irene's address somewhere,' he said suddenly. 'Have a look in my wallet, Sister.'

Surprised, she took it from his locker and handed it to him. After much rummaging around he produced a minute scrap of paper which he carefully unfolded and pressed into Julia's hand. 'Here—that's her address. Well, it was then.' Big, mournful eyes focused on her and she saw that he was near to tears. 'Get in touch with her for me, there's a duck.'

Julia took the paper and smoothed it out. There was an address in Leicestershire but no telephone number. 'I'll have to tell Dr Konrad—he's in charge of your treatment and I can't go behind his back,' she said firmly.

He didn't object to that, and after a few minutes she left him. When she glanced back he was busy with his sketchpad again. Clearly the consultant's blunt speaking had worked!

Feeling guilty because she'd misunderstood, she went in search of Paul. She found him with Sister Greene, their heads bent over a chart spread over Sister's desk.

'Yes?'

She almost flinched, that one word was made as unwelcoming as it was possible to be, and she apologised for disturbing him. When she explained about the step-daughter his gaze softened a little, but not much.

He held out his hand for the scrap of paper, and reluctantly she handed it over. She wondered if she was doing right—after all, she was the one Mr Baxter had asked, and she didn't want him to have another relapse.

'Do you suppose she'll want to see him?' she ventured.

'How the hell should I know?'

The harshness in Paul's voice stunned her, and even Linda shot him a puzzled look.

Gritting her teeth to prevent herself from wading into him in front of the Ward Sister, Julia plucked the address from his fingers. 'Since Mr Baxter asked *me*, shouldn't I be the one to investigate? Perhaps the hospital social worker could drop her a line and I could——'

'Your interest in *my* patient does you credit, Sister Carr,' he said grimly. 'Staff Nurse Black is Mr Baxter's therapist and she has to be told about this new development. We have a system here,' he went on, 'and I cannot and will not allow you to circumvent it!'

Julia's cheeks burned and she was grateful that her colleague had tactfully left the office. 'If I've done—or said—anything to annoy you, Doctor, then I unreservedly apologise. I am *not* the doormat type, though, and I suggest you find someone else to wipe your feet on!'

A reluctant smile touched his mouth, and Julia was lost. He certainly knew how to win battles without exerting himself! She sank down in Linda's comfortable chair and tried to speak calmly. 'Shall I get in touch with this lady or will you and Nurse Black arrange it? I want to do what's best for the patient—I'm not trying to interfere.'

'Sometimes I hate you.' Paul's voice was calm and free from bitterness, but his words stung all the more because of the reasoned tone in which he spoke.

'Do you? Why?' Julia didn't want to know, but the question just slipped out.

He shrugged. 'Because you waste your life yearning for a man you cannot have. Wake up and *live*, Julia!' he commanded.

Amazement robbed her of speech. Then he went on to say that he would contact Mr Baxter's stepdaughter and she could keep the man informed of any developments. He bent his dark head over the chart once again, Sister Julia Carr instantly forgotten, and she walked slowly from the office hardly knowing where she was.

Wake up and live, Julia. You are yearning for a man you cannot have. She pondered those words for what remained of the afternoon. Did he mean John? No, that wasn't likely. She was over her grief now. He certainly could not mean the Registrar—Rob Morland was free, but she didn't yearn for him. He was rather a dear and she enjoyed his company, but that was as far as it went. No, he obviously meant himself. Don't yearn for Dr Paul Konrad, because he isn't available. He's way out of *your* league, Sister Carr. That was what Paul meant. Of course she understood that. But she didn't yearn for him any more than she did for Rob. It was utter nonsense to suggest that she did. Just because she found the man desirable on occasions it did not mean she was in love with him. Far from it. When he chose he could be utterly ruthless and hateful. And he had the nerve to say he hated *her*!

Paul's unit was full up the next time she visited. She went to tell Mr Baxter that they were trying to trace

Irene. He was pleased to see her and she sat by his chair for a little while.

He had a companion in his cubicle now, a Mr Dobson, who was the youngest in the unit at thirty-six. Leaving Mr Baxter in the day-room, Julia returned to the ward to speak to Mr Dobson. He glanced up listlessly at her approach.

'Sorry. Did I wake you?' Julia queried with a smile.

'It's all right. I get so tired. Is that natural?' He peered anxiously at her and she hastened to reassure him. Reassurance, she felt, was what they needed more than anything.

'It's perfectly natural, Mr Dobson. When patients first come in they're dreadfully weary—and ill, too, of course. Far too ill to take much notice of what's going on or to have much of an appetite.'

He nodded lethargically. 'All these tests don't help. I asked for the op,' he went on resentfully, and Julia bit back her annoyance. How could people actually *beg* for a bypass operation? For that was what they did. Just because one or two celebrities had been operated on and were apparently cured, the operation had now become the panacea for all ills in the eyes of some people.

'Wouldn't it be better to see what conservative treatment does for you? Then, if you're no better, Dr Konrad will suggest alternatives.'

'The op will put me right,' he went on, as if she hadn't spoken.

It would be bad for him if she attempted to reason with him, make him see that the cardiac surgeon's scalpel wasn't the answer to every heart condition, so she asked him how the heart trouble had begun.

'I suppose it started at work. I'm self-employed, an electrician,' he explained. 'I began to get tired without any real reason. Then this kind of constricting pain used to come. At first it was only when I did any heavy work, but now . . .' he gave a wan smile, 'it's all I can do to walk about now. The pain comes on even when I'm doing nothing. Just the thought of work brings it on!'

Julia sat by him a while longer, leaving when he drifted off to sleep. He was really poorly and she wondered if even a bypass operation would be in time to cure him. He needed rest and yet more rest, at the very least. Perhaps just being away from his job would help, though as he was a self-employed man the worry of his business must always be there, in the background.

She had almost forgotten Saturday's marathon walk, though Wendy reminded her in time. A great number of people were willing to sponsor her, and she was surprised, not realising how popular she was.

When she voiced her surprise, Wendy said firmly: 'Of course you're popular! Silly girl. I've told you before. I see you're walking with Rob Morland,' she went on, after a significant pause.

Julia eyed her balefully. Wendy's plump, good-natured face was watchful. 'I'm merely walking with him, Wendy. He asked me to—there's no more to it than that.'

'No, of course not,' her friend said soothingly, 'but people are bound to comment on it, Julia. You know the grapevine!'

Dismayed, Julia said: 'You don't think anyone will read a romance into it, do you? I just didn't think. I'll tell him I can't come.'

'Julia! All these people are willing to pay good money! You can't let them down. Anyway, it's for charity,' Wendy went on firmly. 'The Great Chief has agreed to start you all off,' she added craftily.

'Who?' Julia's voice was casual. 'Do you mean Mr Almazan?'

'I do not mean Mr Almazan—you know very well I mean Paul Konrad. He's dishy, isn't he? A pity about his filthy temper.'

'Yes, isn't it.' So Paul was firing the starting pistol. Paul would see her with Rob Morland and assume she was taking his advice seriously. That should please him. It did not please *her*, but it was too late to alter the arrangements. Let Paul Konrad think she was beginning a torrid romance with Rob. What did it matter, anyway?

CHAPTER NINE

IT rained on Saturday, but it was only a light shower, and Julia convinced herself that it freshened the air.

Dr Konrad started the field off, before returning to his weekend duty on Tudor. If he noticed that Rob Morland was holding her hand protectively, it wasn't obvious. Indeed, he scarcely glanced her way.

She might have set out with more enthusiasm if she hadn't seen the woman laughing up at Paul. It was Linda Greene. True, Linda's husband was in the walk—she'd caught a glimpse of him earlier. Linda must have come especially to cheer him on, but at that moment it was the consultant cardiologist who was claiming all her attention, and a tight knot of pain settled in Julia's stomach.

Then they were off, Julia easily keeping pace with Rob. Fortunately the weather had cleared and they set off in weak sunshine. Several of the competitors had brought their dogs along and she wished, not for the first time, that she owned a dog. It wouldn't be fair, since she was working full-time, but one dog in particular caught her eye, a perky little Yorkshire terrier. Although it was so short and delicate-looking, it was a spunky little animal and more than made up for its lack of inches by its energy and enthusiasm for the outing. Its owner was a girl in the Administration Office, and gradually Julia worked her way towards her, leaving Rob to fall into step with one of the nurses.

She couldn't see Paul Konrad taking to such a small dog. He would probably favour an Alsatian, or perhaps a chow—a solitary dog, aloof and friendless, rather like the doctor himself. She stooped to pat the terrier, all the while crying inwardly because of the doctor from nowhere.

She completed the five-mile course, somewhat to her surprise, but was glad of transport back. She sat next to Rob in the mini-bus, but they barely exchanged a word. He had told her off for leaving him, and she resented it. Being deserted for a Yorkshire terrier had hurt his feelings and he made sure she knew about it. Another non-dog-lover, like John, she supposed. They didn't know what they were missing.

They made up once they were back at the hospital, and she accepted Rob's apology gracefully. She was too tired, too upset to argue, in any case. All she wanted was a nice cup of tea, a warm bath and an early night with a good book. The 'good book' would probably be a nursing magazine, since she liked to keep up to date, but if she fell asleep over it, that couldn't be helped. Her car had never looked more welcoming, and she refused Rob's offer of a snack in the hospital canteen. All she wanted was her home.

It was not to be. No sooner had Rob departed than Paul appeared, striding confidently towards her across the car park. Her heart sank. Surely he wasn't going to talk shop now?

'Will an hour be enough? Well?' he barked, when she didn't reply straightaway.

'Enough for what?'

'To get showered and changed. We're dining at the Harlequin,' he announced calmly. Then he glanced at his watch. 'I'll give you a lift home. Come on.' Heedless of curious stares from the other nurses, he took hold of her hand and hurried her over to the Mercedes.

Julia meant to protest, of course she did, but somehow the protest was stillborn. Tired though she was, an evening out with Paul Konrad was just what she needed! Thoughts of an early night with a good book vanished. Tomorrow she would have an early night, but tonight she was dining with her Prince Charming.

She was ready in less than an hour. Paul had left once he had seen her all the way up to her flat, promising to return later. For once, she had a new outfit, a simply-styled dress with short sleeves, the midnight blue colour a perfect complement to her hair. She wore her mother's pearls and her own wedding ring, but no other jewellery. Her hair was swept back into a french pleat, but for one wild moment she contemplated letting her hair down, perhaps in more senses than one. Idly she curled a tendril of hair around her finger, tempted.

She gave in to temptation, and was brushing her hair vigorously when Paul arrived. Face flushed and eyes bright, she hurriedly patted her hair into place, wishing she had left it as it was. True, the long, silky hair made her look about ten years younger. It was just past shoulder-length now. What she didn't like about her new look was that it made her feel vulnerable; young and gauche and unsure of herself, just as if she *was* ten years younger, an almost-seventeen-year-old standing on the brink of womanhood.

Ridiculous rubbish, she told herself, opening the door to Paul's second, impatient-sounding ring. 'Sorry—I wasn't quite ready,' she apologised breathlessly, hoping she hadn't already put him in a bad mood.

He merely smiled, then stood in the doorway, apparently not wanting to come in. He did not appear to notice her hair, or indeed her new dress, and she tried hard not to mind.

Wondering if she would ever fathom this man, she sought for some way of breaking the ice. He did not respond to her efforts at conversation until they were on their way to the restaurant, and by then she was fed-up and looking for any excuse to turn round and go home. Surely he wasn't brooding because she'd gone on the walk with his Registrar?

'For heaven's sake, you told me to!' she snapped, her patience at an end.

The car slowed momentarily as if it, too, was amazed at her outburst. 'I told you to do what, Julia?' Paul asked mildly, just as the Harlequin came in sight.

It was her turn to be amazed, as he drove straight past the restaurant. She plucked at his sleeve. 'Aren't you going to feed me, after all? Paul?'

'I decided upon a change of venue. There is an excellent restaurant in Croydon. I thought we might try that, Julia. Don't fret,' he went on, in a calm, reasoning tone which infuriated her.

'I am *not* fretting!' Stubbornly, she folded her arms and stared out of the window. His husky chuckle did nothing to relieve her feelings. She knew she was behaving childishly, but she couldn't help it. She so wanted the evening to be a happy one. She also wanted him to notice her outfit, the way she'd done her hair. Then she shrugged philosophically. Why should he notice? She could not compare with Rowena Dalton. He wasn't interested in her as a person anyway.

The meal and the surroundings almost made up for his total lack of interest in her as a person. To say the surroundings were sumptuous was going a bit far, but the restaurant was the height of luxury as far as Julia was concerned. Not used to being spoiled, she felt a little ill at ease at first, watching as tall, autocratic waiters glided about. The restaurant was part of a big hotel, though with a separate entrance. Everywhere there was sparkling crystal, snowy white tablecloths, gleaming cutlery. Even the air had an expensive aroma, as French perfumes mingled from the other diners. The clientele were rich, from what she could judge, and she gazed reproachfully at Paul.

'You should have told me we were dining with the quality. I would have brought out my fine feathers!' She summoned up a smile, hoping he would not take her remark too seriously. With Paul Konrad, one never quite knew.

'I thought you *were* wearing your fine feathers.' She was captured by the dark intensity of his gaze, and could not have escaped even if she had wanted to. 'You are a beautiful woman, Julia,' he added, and she coloured.

'Thank you, kind sir,' she smiled, wondering if he knew the effect his words were having.

'That dress looks new.' He leaned forward and lightly touched her cheek. 'You should wear your hair down more often. It makes you seem human.' His smile took the sting out of his words, though they hurt, nevertheless. To him, she was still the starchy Sister Carr, less than a woman.

She scanned the menu, giving it all her attention. There was a good selection of dishes, yet she hadn't much appetite. Why, oh, why did they always quarrel? Couldn't they have an outing, just once, without friction?

She settled for fruit juice and a mushroom omelette —hardly exciting. She could have prepared an omelette at home if she'd really wanted one. Yet it was a light meal, enough to keep her tummy satisfied until Sunday morning.

'After your long walk you should eat more than that,'
Paul said reprovingly when her meal arrived, but she
merely smiled. He ordered steak and a salad, but even
the appetising aroma of the meat did nothing to stimulate her own appetite. She felt cheated, yet she knew he
wasn't to blame. It came from within herself. In her own
mind, she had built up this outing to such an extent that
the reality was bound to be a disappointment. She
wished now she had worn her hair up and had thrown on
the first dress she could find. She had dressed to please
Paul, just as once she had dressed to please her husband.
That was what hurt—he simply did not care.

'Poor Julia,' he murmured, and her head shot up. It
was as if he could read her mind. 'You took great trouble
with your appearance tonight and you are upset because
I did not compliment you.' He smiled lazily. 'You are so
beautiful tonight that I have no words worthy enough.'

'If you were Irish I could say you'd kissed the Blarney
Stone!' she retorted swiftly. 'I didn't take pains with my
appearance for your sake, Paul Konrad!' she hissed
across the table. 'I always look neat and tidy.'

'Yes, of course.' His tone was conciliatory, but a smile
lurked in the depths of his eyes, and her annoyance
evaporated.

'I'm sorry. It seems we can't hold a conversation
without it turning into an altercation.' Julia pushed the
omelette away, scarcely touched, but he pushed the
plate back towards her.

'You will eat every scrap,' he insisted. 'You are too
thin, my Julia.'

Incensed, she wished she had the courage to throw the
food in his face. She could have wept tears of rage. He
had no right to treat her like this! 'I'm not a child!' she
snapped. 'And I'm not hungry!'

Their eyes clashed. Then the ridiculous humour of the situation got to her and her lips curved into a smile. Paul sat back, apparently considering he had won the battle. So he had, for she meekly finished her meal, surprised to find that her appetite had returned. 'That was delicious,' she said, pushing the now empty plate aside. 'Would you have force-fed me?'

He nodded. 'But of course! It would have been a pleasure,' he assured her blandly.

'Rotter,' she said affectionately. Loath though she was to admit it, she had rather enjoyed being bossed just this once. It made her feel young and girlish again. Unconscious of the gesture, she smoothed back a strand of hair from her forehead, then saw his eyes stray to her bright hair.

'It's all my own,' she said lightly. 'No tints or streaks. Nature intended me to be a carrot-top!'

'I would like to wake up and find such a beautiful head on the pillow next to mine.'

'Thank you for the compliment, Doctor!' To cover her astonishment, Julia tried to treat his remark lightly. He did not, of course, mean it. Because she'd shown herself to be upset that he didn't comment on her dress, he was now overdoing it.

'I wish that our circumstances were different, Julia. I wish many things . . .' He gave a curiously Latin shrug. 'You have an all-consuming love,' he went on, 'while I have . . . responsibilities.'

'Don't forget Linda Greene,' she said unthinkingly. 'Or is she one of your responsibilities?'

'Sister Greene?' His expression was astonished.

'You keep taking her out,' Julia said quietly, determined not to be drawn into another quarrel.

'Do I? When does this occur?'

Unsure of herself now, she floundered: 'Well . . . she says you take her out, and I've seen you laughing down at her,' she went on accusingly. 'You were together today, at the start of the marathon!'

'Her husband was taking part. She came to wish him well, then we both returned to duty.' His tone brooked no argument, and for the first time, Julia doubted Linda's word.

'But I thought . . .' she began. Not that it mattered any more. If Linda had lied, it was for reasons best known to herself, and Julia began to wish she had never brought the subject up.

'You thought I was having an affair with Sister Greene? Did you, Julia?' he demanded, and she nodded wordlessly. 'A woman who is employed on my ward,' he went on heavily, 'a nursing colleague—a married nursing colleague. Do you think I am completely without morals?' His eyes snapped at her. 'Because I am not English I have no morals. I am a womaniser. I collect women, do I?'

'No! I'm sorry, Paul. It's got nothing to do with being foreign! I must have misunderstood Linda,' she hurried on.

He raised a brow. 'Did you misunderstand her? I wonder.'

They ate their pudding in silence, an uncomfortable silence. She had made things worse. Linda had led her to believe that Paul wined and dined her, though a moment's thought should have convinced her that this could not be true. But she hadn't given it further thought, simply taking her colleague's word for it. She wanted to believe the worst of him and had done so. Now she felt bitterly ashamed. Yet there was no way she could make amends. To apologise yet again would not do. Anyway, mere words were hopelessly inadequate.

Their eyes met, and perhaps Paul saw in her gaze what she could not put into words. After that, the silence became a companionable one and she felt bold enough to ask him about his life before he came to St Crispin's. She didn't want to hear about Rowena Dalton, nor was she prying into his private life. She was genuinely interested, longing to know more about him, what made him tick, what caused him to be the man he had become —aloof, unpredictable and hard.

'My parents were Polish, but they were uprooted,' he began slowly, his thoughts far from her. 'I was born in Germany and started my medical career there. Then I did post-graduate studies in England and the United States. I am a naturalised Briton, though Lucy was American.' He paused, and Julia begged him not to go on if remembering hurt so much.

'Does it hurt? No, I do not believe it does now,' he went on reflectively. 'The past is dead, Julia. Yet we have our memories—good memories.'

She nodded, then stretched out her hand and patted his arm in silent sympathy, just as she might do for a patient. He covered her hand with his own large one. 'My maternal great-grandmother was Russian. She was born there during the reign of the Czars, of course,' he went on. 'It was a very hard world for the poor—and she was poor,' he told her.

Then the coffee arrived, and Julia thoughtfully stirred hers. His words had conjured up a colourful picture of snow and a harsh, forbidding landscape; of peasants toiling under the burning summer sun of long ago. She had been given a privileged glimpse into his past.

'You see? I am a doctor from nowhere, yet a man from many places, from everywhere,' he smiled sadly.

Their eyes met in silent understanding. As if from a great distance Julia heard the sounds of other diners, cutlery clinking against plates, conversation buzzing, muted laughter, and the occasional bray from the man sitting at the next table. Yet they could have been alone. Suddenly she wanted very much to be alone with Paul for the rest of her life.

She was alarmed by the intensity of her feelings for him, and vowed that he would never know how she felt. If it wasn't love, it was something very close to it, though the closest thing was warm affection, and it certainly wasn't that! It was an all-consuming passion which engulfed her. She needed Paul and wished fervently that he needed her. Only he could quell the fire that raged in her breast, only he could bring complete fulfilment. He'd said that he wanted to wake and find her head on the pillow next to his. Did he, she wondered now, really mean it? If so, she would go into his arms without a qualm.

Her thoughts were in turmoil as they left the restaurant. After her arduous day she wanted to fall into bed and sleep dreamlessly. Tomorrow was Sunday and she could relax. But now, with Paul's nearness doing strange and exciting things to her heartbeat, she wondered if she *would* sleep dreamlessly. She was rather afraid she would dream of tall, dark and ruthless heart specialists!

In no time at all they were back outside her flat, and she wondered if she dared ask him up for coffee. When she suggested it, it was in a voice that sounded unlike her own, and he did not reply for a moment.

Then he said softly: 'Coffee, Julia? Just coffee?'

She avoided his gaze. 'I don't honestly know,' she said. 'Just coffee, I expect.' Her voice quivered, then she felt his hands smoothing back her hair. His fingers deftly entangled themselves in it, pulling her towards him. She rested her head on his shoulder and closed her eyes, weary of constant fighting. She wanted a truce even if it lasted only a short while.

When they got out of the car, they strolled hand-in-hand up to her flat. She fumbled when getting out the key, her palms moist, and Paul had to unlock the door for her.

She left him in the sitting-room, murmuring, 'Coffee,' as she vanished in the direction of the kitchen.

When she picked up the laden tray she felt, rather than saw, the consultant. 'Let me take that, my Julia,' he said softly, and, with a faint sigh, she relinquished her burden.

'I'm not *your* Julia,' she felt bound to say as she held open the door for him. 'Put it on the glass table. Thank you.'

'I wish you could be,' he said as she handed him a cup of coffee with hands that shook ever so slightly.

'Well, I can't! You said you wished circumstances could be different. So do I,' she said sharply. 'You told me to get out and live, and that's what I'm trying to do. Only . . .' She let the sentence trail off, for how could she go on? How could she say 'if only you would let me'?

She sat opposite him, her mug of milk cradled in her hands. When he crossed to her side she tensed, not sure she wanted to cross the last divide, make the ultimate sacrifice.

Carefully he set her mug down on the table-mat, then cradled her face in his strong hands. 'Love me,' he commanded, and, tentatively, wonderingly, Julia reached out to touch his face. She rested her fingers on his harsh mouth, then swayed towards him. Her arms wound themselves around his neck as he pressed his lips against hers.

Waves of passion swept over her and every nerve tingled as he crushed her to his chest, his hands moving lovingly over her body. She moaned with ecstasy as his mouth sought hers repeatedly. Then he nuzzled her throat and she was swept along in a great tidal wave of desire. Paul gently touched her breast, his eyes dark with his longing, his need, which matched her own. She could almost believe herself in love, ridiculous though the idea was.

The settee was only a two-seater, and when he swept her up in his arms and carried her through to the bedroom, she did not protest. Her bed was warm and comfortable, and Paul could achieve his wish of finding her red hair next to his in the morning. He set her down on top of the duvet and she gazed up at him through half-closed eyes. They were in the dark, but he was silhouetted against the light from the sitting-room.

'Yes or no, my Julia?' he asked, his voice tender and loving. He stretched out beside her, close but not touching.

She heard his ragged breathing and knew he was making a supreme effort at control. She also knew she could not go through with this. It was a violation of her marriage vows, to let another man make love to her—a man whom she did not love. Stubbornly she argued with her heart, which insisted that she *did* love him. It was absolute rubbish, her conscience retorted. How could she love a man she scarcely knew, a man with no roots, no home, a man with responsibilities that included Rowena Dalton and possibly her daughter as well?

'No,' she whispered into the darkness, then felt the bed shake as he got up. 'Paul? I'm sorry. I thought I could, but it seems so cold-blooded like this.' Her voice was full of the misery she had caused them both and she doubted if he would ever forgive her.

There was a soft chuckle in the blackness. 'It didn't seem cold-blooded to me!'

Relieved, she sat up, then reached out to touch his arm. 'I wish I could, but . . .' Tell me you love me, Paul. That was what she was really saying. Then it would be all right. If he loved *her*, it would not matter that she could not return the emotion. Mutual passion and his love would be enough. But to make love like this, when neither party was actually *in* love—that seemed morally wrong and against all her principles. Some women could do it, but not her. She hoped he understood.

She felt a light kiss on her brow, then he left her, closing the bedroom door behind him. Julia turned her face to the pillow, waiting until her heartbeat settled back to its normal rate. Crying would help, but no tears came, her anguish was too deep, too painful for that. A knife turned in her heart, the surgeon's scalpel that Paul tried to avoid for his patients.

When she heard the front door close she got up and switched on all the lights. She surveyed herself in the bathroom mirror and knew she looked awful. A dull-eyed, wan girl gazed back at her. There were dark circles under her eyes and her head throbbed. If this was what passion did to a woman she was better off without it!

After a warm bath and a cup of cocoa, she went back to bed, but was still awake when first light showed. She supposed she must have dozed a little but could not remember doing so. Thank heaven it was Sunday!

On Monday Julia walked to work, since her car was still in the St Crispin's car park. It was a beautiful, cloudless morning and so hot that she would have given a fortune to relax in a shady garden beside an equally shady swimming pool, instead of going on duty. She was still dwelling on the pleasant idea when she bumped into Paul Konrad in the corridor—literally bumped into him, since she wasn't looking where she was going. Her face flamed as she recalled the events of Saturday night. Or rather, the *non*-event.

He was grim-faced and looked as if his weekend had been as wretched as her own. 'Sally tells me she is discontinuing her training,' he said without preamble.

Grateful that he did not want to discuss the weekend, Julia murmured: 'I'm sorry.'

'Sorry for what, Julia?' he asked stonily, and her temper rose. He must have been brooding since Saturday night.

'Sorry for everything, Dr Konrad,' she said formally. 'Do you want me to try to persuade Nurse Dalton to stay? I've given the matter some thought.'

'Oh? Which matter are we discussing now?' His voice had an edge, and she wanted to shake him. Couldn't the man see what he was doing to her?

Her mouth trembled. It was wicked and insensitive of him to beat her verbally like this. 'How can you be so insensitive!' she snapped. 'Do you think I enjoyed sending you away? Do you?' No one else could make her suffer as this man was doing. She hoped Mrs Dalton knew what she was taking on.

Paul shook his head, then tenderly reached out and touched her cheek. 'Goodbye, my Julia.' His voice held regret, sadness, too.

He was gone before she fully came to. *Goodbye, my Julia.* Her lips formed the words: 'Goodbye, my Paul'. Paul Konrad was in the past, and she tried hard to kick him out of her mind just as she had unwittingly kicked him out of her life.

Memory of his sad, darkly intense eyes could not be erased so quickly. They came back time and time again to haunt her that morning, and it was with mixed feelings that she saw Sally Dalton approach just before lunch. Sally's set were in school all day and she had meant to tell the girl to come to see her later. But because Sally reminded her so much of Paul she had put off the evil hour.

'Come in, Sally. I hear you're leaving us,' she said without preamble, and the student's brown eyes narrowed.

'Did Uncle Paul tell you? I suppose he must have done. I wanted to tell you myself.' She sat down, clearly ill at ease.

Julia forced herself to smile reassuringly. 'What will you do for a living?' she asked. 'And what about Uncle Paul's unit?'

'Oh, don't!' Sally burst out suddenly. 'I don't want to let him or his patients down—truly I don't.' Her eyes begged for understanding.

'Did you go on Saturday? I'm afraid I was tied up with that charity walk.'

Sally nodded. 'I spent two hours there. I don't mind going by myself now. I got Mr Baxter interested in basketwork.'

Julia looked blank. 'Basketwork? I didn't know you could do that sort of thing?' The hospital Fête loomed large in her mind, and every saleable item would be welcome.

'One of the OTs does alternate Saturdays and we got on famously. I did my artwork, then helped her. Mr Baxter was *almost* enthusiastic. He's keen in spasms, you know,' Sally confided. 'We'll have to take it gently at first.'

The idea that had lurked in the back of Julia's mind grew to fruition. She ought not to mention it without testing Paul's opinion, but after Saturday she felt she could not ask his advice. 'Your interest in art set me thinking,' she began carefully. 'It occurred to me that once you had your nursing qualification you might like to train as an occupational therapist.'

'That's two lots of training, Sister,' the girl pointed out politely.

'I know, but it was just a thought. It's hard work, though. Here,' she handed Sally a leaflet, 'that explains what's required. You would learn anatomy and physiology as well as psychology, psychiatry, and all about the various illnesses and disabilities that the OT can help.'

Sally bent her dark head over the leaflet, and while she was engrossed, Julia played her trump card: 'They might not want you on the course if you throw away your nursing training like this. Apart from the theoretical work, OTs have to do a great many hours of clinical experience—hard practical work, Nurse,' Julia went on. 'Registered nurses are given a concession there, though. They do fewer clinical hours.'

Sally went off with her leaflet and the thoughts Julia had cunningly planted. Of course St Crispin's didn't want to lose the girl, but if she became an OT instead, she might return there to do part of her clinical work. And she would be of invaluable help to Paul in his cardiac unit. It was up to Nurse Dalton to make her own decision. She could do no more.

Later, she went along to see Mr Baxter, keen to hear more about the basketwork. He was reading a newspaper when she arrived, a sign that he was beginning to take an interest in the world again. 'This paper prints photos of missing kids, Sister,' he said, waving it under her nose. 'Do you suppose I could advertise my Irene there?'

She shook her head. 'She's hardly a child, Mr Baxter. Anyway, the hospital social worker has written to her at the address you gave. Let's hope she's still there.'

Julia left him, intending to look in on Mr Dobson, but when she got to the ward after leaving Mr Baxter in the dayroom, Mr Dobson's bed was empty. It was made up as an admission bed with the bedclothes in a pack, and she turned questioning eyes on a passing nurse.

'He died early Sunday morning, Sister. Cardiac arrest,' the nurse said matter-of-factly, and Julia paled. 'We're having a new admission in his bed tomorrow—a Mr Marshall.' She hurried away, leaving a sad Julia to return to the school. Poor Mr Dobson, so young. She wished passionately that Paul could have saved him. Probably the man had been hospitalised too late. No wonder Paul was so haggard-looking this morning! They must have called him out. If it was before daybreak on Sunday then it was a good thing he was at home; he might so easily have spent the night with her.

The following morning Rob Morland telephoned her at the school, requesting her presence with a group of students, on another ward round. A happier Julia decided she would take part of Sally Dalton's set. Being included in a ward round would make them feel important, feel that they were 'real nurses' at last.

In the end, she took five students, but left out Sally Dalton. She always seemed to be shepherding the girl and she could not go on doing so. It was hardly fair to the others in the set, and Sally was leaving anyway. Before the round she gave them a brief rundown of Tudor Ward and what the cardiologist was trying to do there. She also mentioned Mr Almazan's important work performing bypass surgery in cases where conservative treatment did not effect a cure. She kept it simple, and was rewarded by a flood of questions.

She was shepherding her flock along the corridors towards the cardiac unit, when the cardiac arrest bell went. The words 'Cardiac arrest—Stuart Ward' came over the tannoy system, and Julia hurried her group along. They were rather junior to be attending a cardiac arrest and would not, naturally, be expected to assist. But the more emergencies they saw the better, Julia felt. The sooner they came to terms with the sharp end of medicine, the sooner they would be able to assist in emergencies.

They crowded to one side as two porters came hurrying by, hurtling the resuscitation trolley along with them, the 'red devil' as it was known, from its bright red colour. Red devils were kept at various points throughout the hospital ready for a call such as this. Before they reached the ward, Rob Morland raced past them, his bleep still going. Julia did not hurry her group. They must not get in the way of the emergency service, and she wanted to prepare them a little first.

'The resus team includes two doctors,' she explained, before they reached Stuart, 'plus an anaesthetist. He sees to the intubation—that's passing a tube into the casualty's trachea or windpipe, to give access to the respiratory tract,' she added. 'The other doctors may be needed to operate the defibrillator machine. That gives an electric shock to the patient in an effort to stimulate the heart into beating normally.'

She hesitated outside the ward. She could see the

emergency right at the far end of the ward, and it would not do to go trooping in with a load of students. She picked just one girl to take with her, telling the others they must reassure the other patients—a necessary task for which there was not always sufficient staff.

Walking quietly, she and the student went down to the far end where resuscitation was under way. One or two other nurses were gathered there simply to watch and learn so that they could assist in the future. It was the policy at St Crispin's for one nurse from each ward to be allocated to cardiac arrest duties, either to observe, or to assist if the emergency was in a ward or department near them.

If Julia had wondered where Paul was during the crisis, she had her answer. He was at the patient's bedside trying to get a drip into a vein. The nurse assisting him stood holding the bag of infusion, and Julia ran to get a drip stand, annoyed that no one on the ward staff had done so. The nurse couldn't be much help to him if she was left supporting the bag. Julia recognised the woman now. It was Mrs Worth, an obese new admission.

She stood back as the defibrillator was brought into use. Mrs Worth's heart was now beating again, but its beat was feeble and irregular, and therefore unsatisfactory. With such a poor beat, the heart could not do its job adequately. The electric shock from the defibrillator would stop the heart and restart it, this time with a strong, regular beat, assuming she wasn't beyond all help.

Two doctors from the emergency team smeared jelly on to the electrodes, then attached them to the patient's chest. They all stood clear while the shock was given, and fortunately it was successful. Julia would explain all the drama to her girls later on, but hoped the student with her was making mental notes.

Mrs Worth, bed and all, was whisked to ITU, only a very short journey, and Julia signed to her students to follow her out of the ward.

Paul glanced at them as he stood up. 'Is that your group for my ward round, Sister?' he asked, his eyes cold.

'Yes, sir. Shall we go to Tudor now?' she asked meekly, wondering if he might want to put back the round. He needed a few minutes to collect himself. She moved aside as the red devil was wheeled back to ITU for checking.

'Send the students. I'll see you in my office,' he said curtly, and Julia was left staring after him as he left.

She sent the girls on ahead, then made her way very, very slowly towards Paul Konrad's office.

CHAPTER TEN

IT was the first time Julia had been to Paul's office. It was on the other side of Men's Medical. He was gazing out of the window when she tapped at the door, and did not turn at her approach.

Not knowing if she was to be criticised or praised but guessing the former, she sat in the chair he hadn't bothered to offer.

Reluctantly, it seemed, he turned to face her, and his voice was low when at last he spoke. 'Sometimes I wish I had never met you, Julia.'

She knew him too well by now to be surprised at *anything*, so she waited.

'I want to thank you for your assistance,' he went on slowly, his eyes bleak when they rested on her.

'With Mrs Worth? It was little enough,' she assured him. 'I wonder if she'll do?'

He frowned. 'She came through, but I'm not too happy about her. You heard about Mr Dobson?'

'Yes, one of the nurses told me. I was shocked. Did you expect him to die?'

'I never expect patients to die, Julia. One must think positively. But yes, his heart was in a state of turmoil, for want of a better word. His attitude did not help. Like Mr Baxter, he would not relax. *Could* not relax,' he finished, half to himself.

'Ted Baxter is doing well now. Nurse Dalton and the OTs are getting him on to handicrafts.'

'Yes. Nurse Dalton,' he said heavily, 'did you suggest

she might try occupational therapy?'

'She confirmed yesterday that she was definitely leaving,' Julia said calmly. 'I pointed out that if she qualified as a nurse first she could then apply for OT training, if she was still interested. She seems an arty-crafty type, though she would make a good nurse, given time,' she went on more slowly, not sure if that was strictly true.

'Rowena is furious. She wants her daughter to be a nurse.'

'Yes, of course,' Julia said demurely. No way was she going to be drawn into an argument over the wretched girl *or* her mother!

'She is feckless—a sweet child but immature,' Paul continued. His eyes held a burning intensity as they rested upon her, and she knew with certainty what she had suspected for a while now.

'She takes after her father, doesn't she? Keen as mustard for short periods, but unreliable,' she said reflectively.

He nodded, then that sensuous half-smile appeared and she fought to keep the hunger out of her eyes. She wanted nothing more than to please him in any way she could, for she loved the man. She forced herself to admit it at last. She loved a man she could not have.

'Sally's father was a distant cousin and also my best friend. We came to England together. You noticed the resemblance.'

'Yes, I did,' she admitted bitterly, 'then jumped to the wrong conclusion. I'm ashamed of myself. Once I got to know you both better I realised that the likeness was only superficial. She isn't like you in character, in determination, in sheer grit.'

'In stupidity, you mean,' he said gently. 'For I have

been stupid, not seeing what was before my eyes all along.'

Since she did not understand what he meant, Julia could not comment. Instead she rose, reminding him gently of his ward round.

He held out his hand and, wonderingly, she took it. 'I hope we can be friends, Julia. Grant me that at least.'

Taken aback, she could only nod, too full for words. Although Paul was in some way tied to the beautiful Rowena Dalton, he still wanted to be friends, and that pleased her. Anything would be better than this constant bickering interrupted only by the occasional shortlived truce.

They strolled companionably back towards Tudor and the waiting patients. Julia's thoughts were bitter as she reflected on her hastiness. If only she had realised earlier that Sally could not be the child of such a fine man! If only she had realised just how much she loved him, too.

The following morning Rowena Dalton appeared in Julia's office, an enormous diamond sparkling on her ring finger. Since the ring could not be ignored, Julia offered the woman her best wishes. 'Should I congratulate your fiancé?' she went on, her jaws aching with the effort of smiling when she really wanted to cry.

Mrs Dalton gave a coy smile, then put her fingers to her lips. 'Please don't mention it to him. It's supposed to be a secret until my birthday. He doesn't know I'm wearing it, but I just couldn't resist it! See?' She moved her hand this way and that, the beautiful stone flashing and sparkling as she did so.

Julia felt numb as she examined the ring. 'It's very attractive, Mrs Dalton. I expect Sally is pleased?'

'She doesn't know yet, Sister. You mustn't mention it

until Paul and I have had a chance to talk to her,' she begged.

'Just as you wish. Has your daughter mentioned the occupational therapy training to you?'

'Oh, that! Yes, but it's quite unacceptable. She must finish her nursing training!' Mrs Dalton insisted.

'I hope she does, Mrs Dalton. Training a nurse takes a great deal of public money,' Julia said severely. 'I see no reason why we should take someone into training and then let her leave before she's done any real work or benefited herself or the public.'

A surprised Mrs Dalton agreed with that, and assured Julia she would try to make Sally stay. At the doorway she delivered the parting blow, though she might not have realised how much pain it caused. 'I hope you will be able to attend my wedding, Sister. I know how much my daughter thinks of you. Paul, too, of course. He's always saying what a dedicated nurse you are,' she trilled.

With a noncommittal reply, Julia let her out. She felt cold, icy-cold. Yet it was another scorching hot day. She reached for her navy blue cardigan. Nurses weren't supposed to wear cardigans on the ward, but today they would have to make an exception. She felt she would never be warm again.

Because she had a rare afternoon free, she asked Linda if she could take her sketch-pad to Tudor Ward. Linda Greene's smile was shamefaced. 'Of course you can, Julia. You're welcome any time. I suppose you heard about Mike and me getting back together?'

Julia hesitated. 'I know he was on the charity walk and you were there to cheer him on,' she said carefully. 'Paul told me.'

'Paul's been funny ever since—a bit grim,' Linda

confided. 'He says he's been hearing rumours on the grapevine about the two of us and if he finds out who started them, he'll make them wish they'd never heard of him!'

'Yes, I imagine he will,' Julia said evenly. Linda would not be telling any more lies about her relationship with the consultant, that was for sure.

There seemed no logical reason for her colleague to lie, and Julia put it down to pure spite. Linda knew she could not have Paul herself and didn't want anyone else to have a romance with him. Then, too, her marriage had been going through a bad patch. She probably dreamed of a tall, dark and handsome stranger striding into her life, rescuing her from the dreary, everyday round. That was a common enough dream—the dashing knight on a white charger!

Mr Baxter was being put through his paces by a physiotherapist when Julia went in search of him, and she stopped to watch for a few moments. Then she sketched one or two of the others, sitting to talk to them as she did so. Each patient had his or her own therapist, but it relieved the monotony for both sides when a new face appeared, and Julia felt that the art lessons Sally Dalton was giving on Saturdays were a tremendous help. The problem was that once working full-time on the wards, Sally would not necessarily have weekends free. She herself would have to fill the gap for as long as possible. She could help with the wall mural, if nothing else. Sally had started it already with the enthusiastic help of the occupational therapists.

The idea of taking over the art therapy appealed to her. She could always avoid the weekends when Paul was scheduled to be on call. Seeing him, speaking to him in an informal atmosphere, would be painful. It would tear her apart now she knew that there was no hope for her. He was committed to marry Rowena Dalton, who would not, Julia felt, be a suitable wife for him. Though she obviously had money, and that might have swayed Paul. If she was rich enough she might be willing to provide necessary pieces of equipment for his unit. To someone as dedicated to his work as Paul, that would be an important consideration and could not be regarded as mercenary.

Before leaving, she went over to see Mr Marshall, who was occupying the late Mr Dobson's bed. He was in his forties, with a ruddy, weatherbeaten skin. He looked fit compared with some of the others, and she smiled down at him.

After introducing herself she asked if he wanted to be sketched. He turned dull grey eyes on her, then nodded. 'It'll do to give to the wife.'

Julia sketched him in silence, knowing how much he needed rest. Now was hardly the time to ask about his illness. She could always get the details from Linda, but to her surprise, he began to talk. He had had a heart attack some months before. 'Just before Christmas it was, Sister. All that fussing about! Buy this, buy that——'

'I know. It's a rat-race at Christmas,' Julia agreed. 'There isn't much religion in it any more. Have you any children? It's always a puzzle knowing what to buy them.' The hassle over that had helped to cause his attack, no doubt.

There were three children, two teenage boys and a much younger girl. 'She keeps on wanting this, wanting that. Screams something chronic when she doesn't get her own way,' he rambled on. 'I get this tight feeling across my chest, Sister.'

'Like a tight band?' He nodded, and she went on: 'It's quite common, Mr Marshall. Patients often speak of the pain on exertion being like a tight band across the chest, almost as though something was squeezing them.'

'Doc says I can manage without an op.'

'That's encouraging news, anyway. Dr Konrad believes we must always try medical treatment first even when people are determined to have surgery.'

She left him after a few moments. Despite his obvious exhaustion, he was in better shape physically than poor Mr Dobson, and with rest, nourishing fluids and a temporary escape from his demanding family, he should recover. That wasn't the end of the story as far as the unit went, she knew. Once pronounced fit he would be provisionally discharged and followed-up at frequent intervals by Paul or his Registrar. When Paul left, his research finished, another consultant would be appointed to carry the work forward. Patients would continue to be followed-up for a period of several years.

Mr Marshall had an unhelpful family background, Linda told her when she called in to say she had finished. The wife, a heavy smoker, was demanding and quarrelsome. She had a full-time job, whereas Mr Marshall had been laid off after Christmas, and this had led to more friction. Then there were the children. One boy had already been in trouble with the law. This was the family to which the patient would be returning, and it did not take a trained nurse to realise that he was a prime candidate for another, probably fatal, attack.

'So we try to assist him to cope,' explained Linda. 'We can't alter the family, but Paul has seen the wife and explained, rather bluntly, that she and the children were killing her husband!'

'He doesn't mince his words,' Julia agreed, with a sad

smile. She would miss his bluntness, even though she was often the victim of it.

'Of course we try to re-educate the family as well as the patient, but often they're people with no insight,' added Linda, then she shrugged. 'We try, but we can't win them all. Paul says there's no point in us getting uptight about it and becoming stressed ourselves.'

A thoughtful Julia left the ward. She was becoming stressed over Paul, but he would be the first to tell her how dangerous that was. *Her* heart was breaking, but in a different way from those of his patients.

She was in Stuart Ward next day, supervising a student taking a nursing process test, when Paul appeared. Determined to avoid him, she quickly pulled the curtains around the patient's bed. It wasn't necessary, but it shielded her and did not distress the patient in any way. No sooner had the three of them settled down again than a male voice spoke outside the curtain. 'Could you spare me a few moments, Sister Carr?'

Julia sighed. He had eyes like a hawk! Either that or his antennae vibrated just as hers did when he was around!

Excusing herself, she peered out through the curtain, unwilling to step right outside unless it was urgent. She managed a smile for the consultant, but he was not smiling as he waved a letter in her direction.

'It's from Mr Baxter's Irene. She's asked if she can visit him. Shall we tell him together?'

Together. How wonderful that one word sounded to her as she smiled her agreement!

Promising the student and patient that she would return directly, Julia went with Paul to Tudor, where Ted Baxter almost cried with happiness on hearing the good news. A warm glow filled her. Even if she hadn't performed any physical nursing tasks for the man, she could at least take some credit for the stepdaughter's letter. She vowed that if she was free when the woman arrived, she would sketch the two of them so that Mr Baxter had a tangible reminder of Irene's visit.

If she hoped she could now escape from the consultant, she was mistaken. Tudor Ward office was empty, and when they reached it he leant against the door, his face cold. 'Did you find out the reason for your landlord's visit?'

The unexpected question brought sadness to her eyes. Poor Mr Randolph! 'Yes, I did. I've been to see Mrs Randolph again. I nursed her once when I was doing some agency work,' she explained quietly. 'She's bearing up rather well. She said she had known he couldn't go on for much longer. He simply wouldn't diet or give up smoking. He drank a lot, too.'

'A prime candidate for Tudor, then,' remarked Paul, still unbending. 'What *did* he want?' he persisted, and she frowned at him.

'I can't see that it's any of your business, Doctor,' she said, her voice as chilly as his. 'Now, if you'll excuse me, I have a student to assess.'

Without a backward glance, she marched out into the corridor, only to run into Rob Morland. She hadn't seen him for a few days and supposed he must have lost interest in her. She had seen him in the canteen chatting up a pretty nurse, and Wendy told her that she'd seen Rob out on the town with the nurse.

Rob's face lit up. 'Just the girl I've been wanting to see! I've got two tickets for the London Festival Ballet on Saturday—they're touring the area. Like to come?'

Because of Paul's attitude over Mr Randolph, Julia accepted. It was simply an evening out for two lone people. She would encourage Rob to talk about the nurse in whom he now appeared interested. Probably because the girl couldn't go to the ballet he was taking *her* instead! 'I wouldn't have thought ballet was in your line,' she smiled, her voice carrying clearly to Paul, who remained in the office.

Rob chuckled. 'You'd be surprised, my lady! See you!' With a cheery wave he walked into Sister Greene's office, and Julia heard him greet his chief.

Saturday, though Rob could not know it, was her birthday. Twenty-seven was only three years off thirty. Yet women often admitted that, for them, life began in their late thirties or forties, once the children were off their hands and their husbands were established. But I haven't children or a husband! Julia protested silently. My life is finished. Paul is going to marry Rowena Dalton, take on the burden of a stepdaughter, while I have nothing and no one. Of course she was being self-pitying. It was up to her to make the effort, get out and about more. Twenty-seven wasn't the end of the world. Her relationship with Rob Morland could never be more than a friendship, there was no chemistry between them. Nothing like the potent attraction between her and Paul Konrad. Yet there were other eligible men on the staff. She had turned down so many invitations since John's death that she had lost count of them. From now on she must start accepting life instead of rejecting it.

Wendy Hamilton had a carrying voice, and Julia was afraid the whole hospital would hear her rendition of 'Happy Birthday' next morning! 'Friday again,' she trilled as they met in the school. 'A whole weekend to look forward to *and* a birthday tomorrow! Who's a lucky girl, then?'

Julia smiled. 'I am, Sister Hamilton. Though I've enjoyed being twenty-six. It's a pity to give it up!'

'Make the most of your last day at twenty-six, then!' chuckled Wendy. 'Must rush—I've a load of students on Stuart. Happy birthday for tomorrow if I don't see you any more before then!' She whirled out in her usual way, then Julia heard her greet someone. Probably the Tutor, she decided. Glancing at her watch, she realised it was high time she was moving as well.

The carnations arrived the following morning—beautiful hothouse blooms of pink and salmon and a deep, dark crimson. They were placed outside her flat door, professionally wrapped in cellophane. The outer paper bore the name of a local florist, but no one had rung. Julia could not have failed to hear the bell. Two dozen beautiful carnations! They were her favourite flowers, but no one at St Crispin's knew that, not even Wendy. There was no card with them, which made it all the more mysterious. Then she remembered Wendy speaking to someone in the school just after she'd been singing 'Happy Birthday'. It must have been Rob. He was supposed to pop in for details of some lectures he was to give the more senior students. He must have crept out again, not wanting her to know he'd overheard.

Touched, Julia smiled at the flowers, then cradled them to her breast. She must put them in her best vase. In the end they took up three vases because she wanted to display them to advantage.

The doorbell rang just as she was preparing her lunch. She had been out shopping and brought back loads of salad vegetables plus some fruit and coleslaw. She hesitated before answering it. She wasn't expecting anyone and she hoped it wasn't young Sally. She intended to spend the afternoon on Tudor as it was, and she wanted

a little while to herself. Not sure why she was doing it,
she hid the flowers before opening the door to the now
insistent ringing. Probably it was Rob come to wish her
happy birthday, but there was always the chance it might
be Paul Konrad, and she didn't want him to know about
the flowers.

It *was* Paul, and, stubbornly, she decided not to let
him in. He had no right to violate her privacy like this.
She never called at his bungalow, so why should he think
he had the right to drop in whenever it suited him?

'Am I to be kept on the doorstep like a salesman?' he
demanded, his brows meeting in a frown.

'Oh, all right, come in,' Julia said carelessly, going
back to her kitchen and leaving him to close the door. He
followed her into the kitchen and watched in silence as
she prepared herself a colourful salad.

She produced a bottle of white wine from the fridge
—a birthday was a special occasion and she'd treated
herself. Drinking alone was no fun, but the following
weekend Wendy and her husband were coming to
dinner and she could celebrate properly then.

She buttered two crispbreads while she silently wondered whether she ought to invite Paul to lunch. Presum-
ably that was what he had come for, and she *did* owe him
a meal. Her mind made up, she fetched another glass
and held the bottle up invitingly.

'Thank you.' He accepted the glass of wine, then
carried it into the sitting-room, leaving Julia no option
but to follow.

'I hope you like salad.' She perched on the arm of the
settee, well away from Paul, who remained standing.

'Salad?' he echoed. A muscle jerked in his cheek, and
she longed to enfold him in her arms and kiss away the
tribulations of the day.

'That's what I'm having for lunch,' she said instead. 'There's plenty for two, and I owe you a meal, after all.'

'Oh, that.' He made a deprecating gesture. 'Forget it. I have a lunch engagement, anyway.'

That would be with Rowena Dalton. 'That's all right, then.' Her words sounded hollow and unnatural, but she couldn't think of anything else to say. He was, she presumed, taking Rowena to the Harlequin, since it appeared to be his favourite restaurant.

He glanced around the room, then finished his drink. 'No flowers?' he asked suddenly. 'The room looks bare.'

'I'm sorry about that,' she retorted. Then the thought occurred to her that he might know about Rob's flowers. He knew everything, or so it appeared sometimes. She would pretend she hadn't received flowers from his Registrar. 'I'm not a flower person,' she went on, avoiding his eyes. 'Sister Carr is a practical, down-to-earth, *dedicated* nurse. No flowers, no pictures, no mementoes of holidays in Spain or wherever.'

'I see.' He glanced down at the glass as though surprised to find it empty, then took it through to the kitchen. 'Enjoy your salad. Oh, by the way . . .' he hovered in the doorway, 'Sally—she has taken your advice and decided to stay in nursing. I thought you would wish to know. That's why I came.'

'For how long, I wonder?' smiled Julia. 'But thank you for telling me. I hope I haven't kept you?' She desperately wanted to know if he *was* dining with his fiancée.

Paul glanced at his watch before replying. 'No, there is plenty of time. I'm not due there until one.'

Rowena must be entertaining him to a meal at home. Her spirits lifted a fraction. At least he wasn't taking the woman to what she thought of as *their* restaurant!

She spent a pleasant afternoon on Tudor. Mr Baxter had perked up considerably as Irene was due to visit in the evening. Sally had been there during the morning, spreading her own particular brand of happiness. Of the consultant there was no sign, and Julia saw from the duty list that Mr Almazan was on call, together with a general physician. Was Paul, she wondered, spending the evening and night with Rowena, as well as the afternoon? Since Sally lived in the Nurses' Home, it was quite likely he would spend the entire weekend with his fiancée. What could be more natural?

Wishing she did not have to appear bright and cheerful, she hurriedly prepared for her evening out. Then she remembered the flowers and hastily brought them out from the cupboard. Poor things! Lovingly Julia stroked their immaculate petals. It wasn't true what she'd said about not caring for flowers. It was strange Paul should notice—men did not usually pay much attention to those things. But he was, she reminded herself, foreign. Englishmen were still a bit selfconscious about carrying flowers or sending them to their loved ones, but to Continentals it came naturally. Even in Russia and Central Europe . . . Her lips parted in dismay as it dawned on her. Paul had sent those flowers! He must have done. It was the sort of gesture which would appeal to him. No—Julia shook her head—it was Rob Morland. Yet why should Paul mention flowers specifically? And she'd told him she wasn't a flower person!

She had to know for sure, and deliberately she showed the carnations to Rob a little later. He duly admired them, then chuckled. 'You must have a secret admirer, Julia! No one sends *me* bouquets!'

'Here, you can have one for your buttonhole.' She

smilingly offered him a bloom, but he backed away in mock horror.

'Not for me, thanks. It'll look a bit wimpish.'

With a sad smile Julia cut off the head of the best bloom, a deep crimson, and wore it as a corsage. It went well with her navy suit—and she wanted to wear it as close to her heart as possible. She knew beyond doubt now that Paul Konrad had sent the bouquet, and he'd gone away believing she had thrown them in the dustbin. For hurting him like that, she would never forgive herself.

She hoped he might forgive her when, somehow, she managed both an apology *and* an explanation of her peculiar behaviour. With Paul one never knew.

CHAPTER ELEVEN

It was after ten when the ballet finished. They had a meal first, Julia insisting on paying. It transpired that the tickets for the ballet had come from Mrs Buss, one of Rob's patients. 'She's got a soft spot for me!' he chuckled as they drove back along the main road.

Julia didn't like to ask why he wasn't taking his pretty nurse friend. It was enough that they could spend a pleasant evening together, a far cry from the emotional upheavals which accompanied an evening with Paul Konrad! She was about to comment on the ballet when, glancing over to her left towards the railway, she saw brilliant lights.

'Rob, look! I think there's been a crash!' The Registrar stopped the car, then they ran back to where the ground dipped and they could get a clearer view. There was a field between the road and the railway line, Kessett station being some half a mile to the east.

'You're right—I can see a carriage lying on its side,' Rob muttered, and Julia gasped in horror. The scene was illuminated by huge arc lights, and there appeared to be crowds of people there. The crash involved two trains, that much was evident.

Julia's heart began an erratic beat as it struggled to break free. It was all so like the rail crash which killed John. She turned away, burying her face in her hands. Her body began to tremble violently with shock, and for a moment she lost control. Then she plucked at Rob's arm. 'Quick! We can turn off at Shepherds Lane—that's the nearest to the line.'

She ran back towards the car, closely followed by Rob. They were soon closer to the railway line and could see figures running about, ambulances, police cars and fire engines. It looked much worse than the crash in which Julia had been involved. Then, her husband had been the only fatality, but from the number of stretchers being carried to the waiting ambulances there appeared to be many serious injuries here and probably a greater loss of life.

Gingerly, they made their way down and introduced themselves to the police officer co-ordinating the rescue work. He directed Rob towards a group clustered near the front of the train, and the Registrar hurried away.

One train, Julia was told, had apparently hit an obstacle on the line, swerved, tilted, then the first three carriages had left the track. The London train, travelling in the opposite direction, hadn't been able to stop in time and its driver's cab had gone into the local train. Both drivers were dead and one passenger, and there were several serious injuries.

Her fear and shock forgotten, Julia assisted where she could. There were enough medical and nursing staff sent from St Crispin's and the Regional Accident Unit to cope with the injuries, so she spent her time comforting the other passengers, most of whom were suffering from some degree of shock.

'It was terrible, Nurse,' one woman told her, clinging to Julia's arm for support. 'One minute we were going along nicely, then there was this dreadful noise and the train stopped and swayed a bit. That must have been when those carriages left the line.' With a hand that shook visibly she pointed up the line. 'I was in the next carriage, thank God!' She began to sob, and Julia supported her as best she could. It all brought back so many memories she had thought buried for good. Darkness had brought a chill to the evening, and she was shivering as much as any of the passengers.

Yet in caring for the less fortunate she could forget many of her own problems, and she had no more time to dwell on the past.

Thinking she ought to help Rob if she could, she made her way towards the main disaster area, carefully avoiding the bits of glass from the smashed carriage windows. Here and there, too, were personal items, and she picked up a teddy bear. There was a small boy among the non-injured, she knew, and she hoped fervently that he was the only child involved. At this time of night the passengers would be mainly folk returning from a day in London or the coast.

Julia couldn't see Rob anywhere, but suddenly she came face to face with Paul Konrad. They stared at each other in surprise, then he gave a strained smile. 'I'm glad to see you, Julia,' he said quietly before turning away as someone called.

A fireman warned her not go any closer. There were at least two casualties still trapped in the wreckage, and it was proving difficult to get them out. The carriages were balanced precariously on the slope that led down to the marshes. One false move and the train would go rolling down, killing any who remained alive inside. A tiny Filipino nurse and their cardiac surgeon, Mr Almazan, also a small person, had volunteered to crawl into the wreckage as far as possible, and Julia's heart was in her mouth as she watched.

Mr Almazan signalled that he'd found someone alive,

then, to Julia's horror, Paul Konrad began crawling under the train, a fireman close behind.

'No, Paul, don't!' she whispered into the night, but no one heard her plea. Paul, being a big man, could not get as far as the others without endangering everybody's lives, but his strength would be useful when it came to lifting any casualties.

She could not bear to watch the man she loved risking his life, and she turned towards the next carriage where firemen were just bringing out a casualty, a woman of about her own age. She was glad to be of use, helping the doctor examine the casualty, who had a fractured femur plus numerous cuts where she had been caught by the shattered glass. She was conscious, though, and appeared to have no serious injuries.

Then, worried sick about Paul, a dishevelled Julia forced herself to seek him again. She began to get agitated because there was no sign of him, but they were lifting a stretcher out of the carriage under which she had seen him crawl. Nearby, someone spoke admiringly of a doctor who had steadied part of the wreckage by sheer brute strength, enabling a smaller doctor to get to a severely injured casualty. 'Big bloke he was—sounded foreign,' an ambulance man said to his colleague as they passed Julia, and she turned frightened eyes towards the wreckage, willing Paul to get out alive.

Then she was pushed from behind and half dragged away as someone shouted that the train was moving. Paul was trapped! She was going to lose her new love just as she had lost the old one! She began to fight them, trying to get to the carriage. Then there was an ominous rumbling as the carriage began to move again.

The last words she heard were: 'Did that foreign bloke

get out? Can't see him anywhere.' Then blackness closed mercifully in on her.

She was forced to spend what remained of Saturday night in hospital under observation. She had suffered a severe emotional shock, and was also bruised and grazed where she had become entangled in the wreckage.

By Sunday morning, when she was discharged, she knew that Paul had escaped from the moving train. It was a narrow escape, according to Wendy Hamilton, who drove her home. Wendy didn't want to leave her, but Julia insisted. As long as Paul was alive and un-injured, nothing else mattered. She just wanted to be alone with her tumultuous thoughts and her memories.

Because it was a beautiful day, a true summer's day, she decided to stroll on the Downs as she did so often when troubled. Then she thought with longing of the peace and tranquillity surrounding Paul's bungalow. She did not feel up to driving and his home wasn't on a bus route. She could hardly roll up in a taxi! In any case, Rowena was bound to be there. Naturally she would wish to comfort her fiancé after his lucky escape.

In the end Julia settled for a bus ride, to within a couple of miles of her favourite patch of Downs, then walked from there. She wished she had a dog to exercise. It would have been protection, too, because it was lonely up on the Downs. Then she passed a few Sunday walkers. They were all couples, which did nothing to ease her heartache. She passed the outcrop of rock where she had first seen Paul with Rowena Dalton and the girl she had presumed was their daughter. Today there was no wind, and she sank down on to the warm grass, leaning back against the protecting rock.

Overhead a few wisps of cloud hung suspended from

the brilliant azure sky. Idly her eyes followed a swift as it dipped and swooped against the heavens. Then she closed her eyes momentarily, lulled half to sleep by the utter peace of the scene.

Before leaving St Crispin's she had enquired after the casualties. Apart from the drivers there was only one other fatality. When Julia enquired about the teddy bear she had put down in order to help with the injured, she was told that it had been reunited with its small owner. The carriage which rolled down the embankment just before she blacked out was, fortunately, empty by then, but Paul and the fireman had got out only just in time.

Although she had damaged her suit beyond repair, she had lost her precious carnation. The beautiful crimson bloom must have fallen out of her lapel. There was still the rest of Paul's flowers to enjoy, though. Smiling a little, she drifted off to sleep.

She awoke at some sound. Alarmed, she sat up, then saw what must have been a dream. Paul Konrad was sitting a few feet away, her carnation cradled in one hand. Julia shook her head to clear it, then peered at him. He certainly looked real enough.

'Paul?' she said tentatively, then he smiled lazily and she knew it was no dream.

He strolled over to her, then sat down by her side. She lifted her face to his, her eyes wide with happiness. 'You rescued my flower!'

'So I did. Here.' Gently he threaded the stem of the sorry-looking bloom through the buttonhole of her sleeveless cardigan.

His face was scratched, but otherwise, he told her, he had escaped injury. He looked tired and drawn, though, and there was a depth of sadness in his eyes. They sat companionably for a while longer, watching the birds.

An inquisitive blackbird eyed them from the safety of a nearby bush, and Julia wished this idyllic episode could go on for ever. But it could not, and when Paul rose and suggested he give her a lift back, she got up immediately, not wanting him to know how much she yearned for his strong arms to enfold her, keep her from further harm.

Protectively, she stroked the wilting carnation, then remembered that she had not thanked him for the bouquet. When she did so, haltingly, he merely smiled. Seemingly the matter was of no importance to him now.

'How did you find me here?' she asked. 'I must have dozed, and when I woke up and saw you, I thought I was dreaming!'

'We met on the Downs once before,' he reminded her. 'I felt that you sought the peace of the hills whenever you were troubled. It is, perhaps, a way of communicating with your husband,' he went on softly. 'You must have shared many happy hours here.' He made a sweeping gesture with his hand, embracing the soft green hills, the distant villages, the sparkling waters of the river.

Julia nodded, too full for words. How could she tell him that she had sought relief up here from her hopeless love for him? There was still Rowena Dalton.

'How is Rob Morland?' he asked, as he drove her back.

'Rob? Oh!' In her fear for Paul's life she hadn't thought to ask about Rob! 'I . . . I didn't think. I just assumed he was all right.' She turned anxious eyes on the consultant. 'Was he injured?'

Paul frowned. 'No. He did sterling work. It was a good thing you were passing at just the right time.' There was a heavy pause, and she waited, wondering if she was to be censured yet again. 'I imagined he went home to your flat last night. That's why I was surprised to find you up here alone.'

'I spent last night in Sick Bay,' Julia said tartly.

'I know,' he admitted. 'When I came to see you, that dragon of a Home Sister said you were sleeping and that not even Royalty would be allowed to disturb you!'

'You came to Sick Bay? No one told me,' exclaimed Julia, her voice full of wonder. He cared enough to visit! 'Where did poor Rob go, then?'

His voice was strained when he replied. 'Someone told me he'd gone to his girl-friend's home for what remained of the night.'

The mists cleared, and she smiled. 'That would be the little blonde from Men's Medical. Rob fancies her, though I'm not sure he realises it.'

'Why did he take *you* out, then?' Paul sounded astonished, and she hastened to explain about the ballet tickets.

'I suppose she either couldn't make it or she doesn't like ballet. Or perhaps he used me to make her jealous,' she suggested. It didn't matter either way. She had had an evening out, which was enjoyable until they had come upon the tragedy. 'You told me once that if I ever came upon another rail accident I would forget my fear,' she went on, wonderingly. 'You said I was a healer and would put the welfare of others first.'

'And so you did. You did not let me down, Julia.'

It wasn't 'my Julia' this time, she noted. She would never be his Julia again, she realised that. She also realised something else. They were outside his pretty home—and yes, there was the same horse staring at them from across the road. 'Will it be all right? My being here, I mean,' she hurried on, when Paul turned his quizzical gaze on her.

'You have my permission to stay for a while,' he teased.

Wondering uneasily if Mrs Dalton would turn up and spoil the day as she had once before, Julia followed him round the side of the bungalow. In the sun lounge, the table was set invitingly. 'No doubt you would like tea?'

'No doubt,' she smiled back.

Later, after two cups of tea and a slice of Austrian torte, she half dozed in the comfortable chair. It was rude to doze in someone else's house, but she needed several hours of deep, dreamless sleep before she could once again become her usual brisk, matter-of-fact self.

'What *did* your Mr Randolph want?'

'What? Mr Randolph?' Crossly she sat up. 'You might have let me sleep, Paul! What about him?'

'When he died, he had called to tell you something of great importance,' he said patiently.

'Oh, that. Yes. The end of my tenancy is nigh!' she said lightly. It would be a blow having to move. The flat had become home. When her mother died she had sold her mother's house, not wanting to be so far from St Crispin's. The flat suited her better, anyway. With Mr Randolph dead, the business would pass to his widow and daughters, and Julia knew they wanted to sell up. She explained all that to Paul. 'He came to tell me that business wasn't so good and he would have to sell the house. His staff had been found alternative accommodation, but I would have to make other arrangements.'

'And what will you do?' He relaxed in the chair opposite, eyes watchful.

'I expect I shall find another flat. I don't particularly want to move back into the Sisters' Home. I like my independence.'

'So you do,' he agreed gravely. 'I was forgetting. You

are Miss Julia Fight-my-own-battles Independence. Yet sometimes I catch a glimpse of a different Julia.'

'Not often, I hope!' she said lightly. Once or twice he had caught her in a vulnerable state, but she was determined that he would never see her cry again or behave foolishly. She patted her carnation affectionately. 'I must go. Shall I get a taxi, or will you be kind and drive me home?' She stood smiling down at him, her eyes suspiciously bright. How difficult it was to hide one's love. How terribly difficult!

When his arms opened invitingly, all her good intentions vanished, all her resolutions, and with a sob she clung to him as if her life depended upon it. 'I . . . I'm sorry,' she said, wiping away the tears that came from nowhere. 'It's just reaction—the shock of the crash and everything. I'll be all right.'

'Will you, my Julia?' he said fondly. 'I expect it brought back memories you had buried deep within. Yet that is a good thing. It is healing to cut away the debris of the old wound. Now you will be strong again. You are over your grief now, perhaps?' he suggested, stroking her hair as she snuggled against his chest.

'Perhaps. In a few years,' she lied. 'Well, I'd better go now—Mrs Dalton might come.'

'Yes, so she might,' he agreed, making no move to stop her as she reluctantly left the comfort of his lap.

He drove her back in silence. Once he had set her down outside the house he sped away, and she supposed he was going to pick up Rowena.

That episode was at an end. He would go ahead and publicly announce his engagement soon. Somehow she must grin and bear it, keep going one day at a time, and not let the world see her agony. She only wished he had chosen a worthier woman.

On Monday morning it was business as usual, even though Julia had been offered a day's extra leave to fully recuperate. Rob was on duty, too, and she paid a brief visit to Tudor Ward to make sure he was all right.

The unit was a hive of activity, and she stayed to have a look round before leaving. They had one vacancy now, Rob told her. 'For how long, I can't say. The Chief is talking about expanding the unit—says he doesn't think we've got enough beds.'

'He may be right. I can see that there's a demand for a unit like this.'

'We haven't the facilities the London hospitals have, unfortunately,' Rob went on. 'More money would be useful.'

His words stabbed Julia in the heart. More money might well be forthcoming from the consultant's fiancée once she became his wife. Paul would be willing to sacrifice his freedom for the sake of the cardiac unit; she knew him well enough by now to realise that.

She turned away, sick with despair. Then Ted Baxter actually waved to her, and she went over to be regaled with the tale of his Irene's visit—the first of many, he expected.

Julia left as soon as she reasonably could, filled with a sadness which she felt was too great to be borne.

Sally Dalton had told her earlier that morning that it was her mother's birthday, and on Rowena's birthday the engagement was to be announced.

When she saw Paul moving purposefully towards her, immaculate and aloof in dark grey suit and silk tie, Julia got her congratulations in first. She owed him that much. If only Rowena would make him happy!

He looked blank. 'I haven't asked yet, so how can I be congratulated on a satisfactory answer to my request?'

Without waiting for a reply, he caught hold of her hand and led her like a child to his office.

Aware of the curious looks they were attracting, Julia struggled to free herself, her face flaming. 'Paul!' she protested, then protested even more as she was unceremoniously pushed into a chair.

'I could not sleep last night,' he said stonily, while she turned her big eyes on him in surprise, wondering what on earth was coming next. 'I wanted to put you across my knee and beat you!' he exploded.

When he was angry, his accent became more pronounced, and Julia liked the sound of it. It was a very sexy accent.

'You have grieved enough. Now you must love me instead of a ghost from the past.'

'But Mrs Da . . .' she began.

'Do you deny you are beginning to love me a little?' Paul demanded. 'I have taken second place long enough, waiting for you to get over your natural grief, as I have got over mine. Then, when I thought we could be lovers, you turn to my Registrar!'

'No, I didn't! It was only a friendship,' she protested wonderingly. 'I didn't know you were interested in me. At least, I *did*.' She coloured, recalling the night she had so nearly given in to her own passion as well as his. Then she remembered the all-important question.

'What about Rowena Dalton, anyway?' she demanded, the laughter leaving her.

'Yes, my Julia? What about her?' Paul said softly.

'It's her birthday, and *you* were to be her birthday present!' she burst out. 'She said you were going to announce the engagement on her birthday. Why, you even gave her a ring!'

'Did I? When?'

His expression was so astonished that she knew the woman had lied. 'An enormous diamond. She kept moving her hand so I could see the stone flashing,' she went on resentfully.

'Ah, I see! That solitaire was her engagement ring from her husband—her estranged husband,' he added. 'Rowena is not yet free to marry again. I do not deny that we had a torrid affair, but it passed long ago,' he said casually.

A flicker of annoyance crossed Julia's face. 'Perhaps any "torrid affair" you had with me would soon pass? Distance lends enchantment to the view,' she added bitterly.

'Does it, my Julia? I think seeing you in my bed and by my side for the rest of my life will be more enchanting than seeing you across a field,' he said seductively, moving towards her.

She swallowed nervously. This was too deep for her. 'I'd better get back, Paul, I—Oh!' His arms and lips very effectively prevented her from getting back, and it was some time before she could find breath enough to speak.

'I love you, Julia, and I want you to be my wife. I hope one day you will be able to love me,' he said gently, his fingers on her lips.

Julia kissed his fingers, her eyes smiling at him. 'I've always loved you, though I didn't realise it until recently,' she admitted.

'Can this be true?' The uncertainty in his voice was more than she could bear, and they clung to each other for comfort.

The doctor from nowhere had found a home and so had she. Out of their shared grief, Julia felt, would come a love so strong that nothing could part them. As she raised her face for his kiss, she knew she had found paradise.

Doctor Nurse Romances

Romance in modern medical life

Read more about the lives and loves of doctors and nurses in the fascinatingly different backgrounds of contemporary medicine. These are the three Doctor Nurse romances to look out for next month.

THE KISS OF LIFE
Sarah Franklin

THE DOCTOR OPPOSITE
Barbara Perkins

TERRITORY NURSE
Judith Worthy

Buy them from your usual paperback stockist, or write to: Mills & Boon Reader Service, P.O. Box 236, Thornton Rd, Croydon, Surrey CR9 3RU, England. Readers in South Africa-write to: Independent Book Services Pty, Postbag X3010, Randburg, 2125, S. Africa.

Mills & Boon
the rose of romance